WHEN THE PARTY DIED

A BROCK & POOLE MYSTERY

A.G. BARNETT

 ODDMOOR PRESS

MAILING LIST

G et FREE SHORT STORY ***A Rather Inconvenient Corpse*** by signing up to the mailing list at agbarnett.com

CHAPTER ONE

"Do you think they'll remember to let him out after he's had his dinner?"

"Yes, Sam," Laura replied, sighing.

"That's if they even remember to give him his dinner," Sam Brock grumbled.

"For goodness' sake!" Laura snapped. "He will be fine; he's four months old now, which in dog years makes him about twenty!"

"It would make him two, actually," Brock replied. "Anyway, you know what your parents are like. I went around to their house and found the front door wide open the other day, and they'd gone out!"

"We've done that at least twice as well, Sam," Laura said. "Now can we try and at least pretend that you want to be coming out tonight?"

Brock felt a stab of guilt.

Tonight was the grand unveiling of a new exhibit at Bexford Museum. Which, along with this being its one-hundredth-anniversary year, had prompted a party. Which was why they now strolled through the centre of Bexford, in the glow of the afternoon summer sun. The yellow stone that the town was built from reflected the warm orange light around the streets, giving the place a surreal quality.

"So, tell me about this new totem pole then," Brock said, looking down at the leaflet in his hand.

"You mean tell you again?" she said, giving him a look that could have melted steel. "Well, like I said to you the other day when you were so clearly listening to me, it's a mortuary pole."

"A mortuary pole? What on earth's that?"

"They were carved when someone important in the community died. Sometimes, like ours, they had the ashes of the person in a small door at the back."

"So it's like a giant wooden gravestone and grave in one?"

"Yes, Sam," Laura sighed.

"Are you OK?" he said as they reached the path that led off the road and towards the museum.

"Yes, fine. Just got a lot on my mind, that's all."

"It's all going to be great," Brock said. "Try and enjoy yourself."

They climbed the shallow, well-worn steps that led up to the arched doorway and were greeted by a young, pale woman with jet-black hair and eye makeup so dark it made Brock think of a panda.

"Hi Laura," the girl said, flashing a grin that contained a pierced upper lip.

"Hi Nancy, has anyone turned up yet?"

"Only Byron and Jemima," she said, grinning. "Don't worry, it's early!"

"I know, I know!" Laura said, taking the brochure that

Nancy handed to her and passing it to Brock. "This is my husband, Sam. Sam? This is Nancy."

Brock grunted a greeting at the young woman, who returned the noise with a suspicious look.

"Oh, right," she said with barely disguised disdain.

Brock noticed that Laura was smiling as they moved through the hallway towards the main building.

"What was that about?" Brock asked. "She couldn't have been frostier if she'd been sitting in the freezer."

"Nancy's not a big fan of authority," Laura said, still smirking. "She's got a lot of rebelling to get out of her system. She's a bright girl though, she wants to get into science."

Brock was about to ask at what time he could expect a glass of bubbly and some food when the sound of arguing echoed around the high stone walls.

"I'm well aware that this place doesn't run on hot air," a well-spoken female voice said in a sharp tone. "But what's the point in us being here if we're not trying to get the best pieces we can and display them?!"

They stepped into the enormous main room of the museum and saw a tall, slim figure standing in the middle of the main central aisle.

The room was bathed in the same golden light they had walked in outside. It filtered down through the glass roof whose frame was built from solid iron and covered with ornate mouldings of flowers and depictions of animals.

"We'll talk about this tomorrow," the woman said angrily. She pressed her thumb onto the screen of the phone to hang up and then stared at it as though it had personally offended her.

"Everything OK, Jemima?" Laura said as they approached.

"Oh, you're here!" Jemima said, turning. The annoyed expression on her face vanished to be replaced by a broad smile.

The two women embraced, kissing air on either side of their cheeks as Brock waited in dread for his turn.

He had always hated the continental habit of kissing people on both cheeks. He found it even stranger when he was expected to kiss a woman on the cheek and then shake the hand of a man standing next to her. On the continent, of course, they kissed everyone. But the British weren't quite ready for that, and so had adopted this strange hybrid that left the inspector never quite knowing what he was supposed to do.

Jemima left him in no doubt though, grabbing him by his broad shoulders and air kissing loudly to either side of his face.

"Nice to see you again," he said gruffly.

"So, is everything OK? Sounded like a bit of a heated conversation," Laura said, her face still concerned.

"Oh, yes," Jemima said. "Just the usual, you know, I think if Byron and I didn't argue at least once a day we'd both go mad!"

Laura laughed. "More like every hour for us," she said, linking her arm through Brock's and giving it a squeeze to let him know she was joking.

"Well, the catering team are all ready," Jemima said, looking over her shoulder. "I've left them filling the last of the serving trays and opening the champagne."

"Is the band here?" Laura asked.

"Yep, they've already sound-checked and are now sampling the canapés. We're all ready!" she said enthusiastically. "Now all we need is people to show up."

"Well, we've got half of my station coming so they should make up the numbers," Brock said.

"They'll definitely put a dent in the champagne at any rate," Laura said, smiling. "So, is there nothing else to help with?"

"No, you've done enough all week. Why don't you go and show Sam the mortuary pole?"

"Will do, give me a shout if you need anything."

She pulled Brock along down the central avenue of the room where pathways set off left and right between rows of displays.

"Come on then," Brock said, hitching his suit trousers up. "Give me the lowdown on this pole's history and why it's such a big deal."

"Well, mortuary poles are the rarest kind of totem pole. Like I said before, they were basically a kind of tomb with a recess that the body or ashes could be buried in."

"And does yours have a body in it?"

"Sadly, no."

He looked at her, his eyebrows raised.

"I just mean it would be a better find for the museum that's all, but there was nothing in ours."

"Where did you find it again? Some manor house, wasn't it?"

"Otworth Manor. It was in one of the barns on the estate, been there decades apparently. The Pentonvilles have lived at the manor for centuries and some ancestor of theirs brought it back from Canada at some point. We're still looking into it. Anyway, William Pentonville died a few months ago, and this piece came to the museum."

"Well it's bloody impressive," Brock said as they reached the base of the wooden pole. The main trunk of it was carved into two large figures, each with a smaller figure on its lap. A second carved trunk ran across the top of the pole to form a "T" shape; it too was ornately carved, but this time with a single figure.

It was roughly fifty feet high, reaching up to the second floor of the building, which consisted of a balcony that ran around the entire room.

"So, this Pentonville chap just left the totem pole to the museum?" Brock asked.

"I think so, yes. Why?" Laura said, recognising the glint in Brock's eye.

"Just odd, isn't it? I mean, why this thing in particular? Especially if it had just been stuffed in some barn for years. There must have been other stuff there that the museum could have benefitted from, not just this."

"Can you just turn yourself off for one moment? Not everything needs an investigation."

"Sorry," Brock said, somewhat surprised by her reaction. He pulled her towards him. "I'm proud of you, you know? This stuff is amazing."

"Sam," she said softly, looking down at her own shuffling feet.

"What is it?" he asked, suddenly concerned. Laura was never nervous like this. She was the one who always had everything together.

"Just wait here a minute," she said suddenly, turning and heading back the way they had come.

Brock stared after her. She had been in a strange mood all day and for some reason, she was putting him on edge.

He turned slowly and looked back up at the totem. The thing was somehow beautiful and ugly at the same time.

He heard voices echoing in the large room behind him

and turned to see the group from the station approaching. They were an odd bunch, seen from a distance.

Daniel Davies was on the left; a tall, gangly lad whom he was fairly sure had an ancestor who was a pencil. Next was Roland Hale, an overweight, small-eyed man who had a sense of humour that centred around irritating other people. Then there were Sanita Sanders and Guy Poole. He noticed how closely they walked to each other, their arms in danger of brushing together at every step. Ah, young love, he thought.

"Hello, sir," Poole said as they arrived. "We're a bit early, but we were told you were down here."

"Is this it?" Roland said, looking up at the totem behind them.

"It is," Brock said, turning and looking at it. "What do you think?"

"I think it's blooming ugly," Roland replied. "What's the point of it?"

"You bury someone important in it, apparently."

"Blimey," Roland said. "Just set me on fire and go and have a pint. Don't bother carving anything."

"Thanks," Poole said. "Duly noted." He turned to Brock. "Where's Laura?"

"Nipped to the loo I think." Brock's eyes twinkled in the dim light of the museum. "Shall we sneak up to the next floor and have a look at where the body goes?"

There was a chorus of approval, and the group moved towards the lift. They squeezed into it, with Roland taking up more than his fair share. They arrived at the mezzanine level with its bizarre arrangement of weapons, voodoo dolls and shrunken heads.

The local kids liked to spread rumours that they were specifically the heads of schoolchildren, shrunk by a former deranged teacher of the local school. The truth was they were long-forgotten tribesmen from South America, but the stories were somehow more fun.

They moved around until they were level with the top of the pole's crosspiece and stared at it. It ran right up against the gangway, and Poole ran his hand over the smooth surface of the wood.

"Not much from the back, is it?" Davies said.

He was right. The back of the pole was a flat plane of wood with no sign of the decoration on the other side.

"I guess people aren't meant to look at this side," Poole said. "Is that where the body was kept?" he said, pointing towards a crack in the horizontal section of the pole which formed a perfect rectangle.

"Looks like it," Brock said, leaning over. He frowned as his eyes focussed on the upper line of the panel. "Someone hasn't been very careful with it," he said, standing up. "Look at those chips in the wood."

Poole leaned over with the others.

"Looks like someone's used a crowbar on it," Sanita said. "Was there anything in it when they opened it?"

"No," Brock answered thoughtfully. Something was coming back to him from when Laura had been talking about this piece a few days ago. "I'm not sure it was the museum who opened this though," he said, running his large hands over the fresh marks in the wood.

"What do you mean opened it?" Laura asked from behind the group. She was heading from the elevator with a frown.

Brock turned to her. "Laura, did you say that the museum never opened this panel?"

"Of course not, we didn't want to damage it. When we

went to see it at the manor, we took ultrasound equipment to check there was nothing in there. Why?"

She moved past him to the edge of the railing and looked across at the pole, her hand reaching out immediately to the cuts in the wood. When she turned back to them, her face was pale. "Sam, we never opened that panel, and it wasn't like that when we looked at it at the manor. There were no chunks out of it like this."

"When was that?"

"On Wednesday."

Brock nodded and turned back to the pole. He reached out and knocked on the wood. The sound came back with a dull noise. He continued knocking, moving his hand along the wood until the noise changed and became lighter. He turned to Laura as he moved his hand back and knocked where the sound became muffled.

"There's something in there."

"There can't be!" Laura said, shaking her head.

"Those marks show that someone tried to open this," Brock said, pointing to them. "You said the ultrasound showed it was empty, so if it's not empty now, then whoever tried to open this must have succeeded and put something in it."

"But why would—" Laura began and then stopped, turning to her husband.

Brock took a deep breath and turned to the rest of the group. "Poole, Sanders, stay here and make sure no one comes near this thing. Davies, Hale, get down to the bottom and make sure no one comes up in the lift or the stairs."

He watched the two young officers nod back at him. "Well, go on then!" he prompted. They jumped into action, as though someone had jerked them on a piece of string.

Davies headed off with his gangly, awkward gait and Hale next to him with his tubby waddle.

"We need to get this panel open," Brock said, turning back to Laura who was still standing in shocked silence.

"Where's your caretaker chap? Frazer, isn't it?""

"Yes." She nodded, her brow furrowed. "He'll be in the basement, I'll come with you."

They headed towards the lift and stepped inside in silence. Brock half turned to her, and she folded her arms, staring resolutely ahead.

"Is everything OK?" he asked.

She sighed. "No Sam, everything is not OK. Someone's chipped our new bloody exhibit and hidden God-knows-what inside it."

"Well, yes," Brock said, turning to her. "But you just seem, I don't know. Like there's something else going on."

She snapped to him, and he saw tears in her eyes. "Yes, there's something else going on!" she screamed at him as she rooted around in her handbag. Brock stared at the brown leather accessory with suspicion. Laura's wretched bag had always held a certain amount of fear over him. When on the odd occasion she asked him to find something in it, it was all he could do to not come out in cold sweats. The thing was a labyrinth of bits and bobs and you could be stuck there for hours looking for the desired object.

She pulled her hand out and held up what looked at first like a pen. He frowned, and peered closer as the lift pinged, and the doors began to open.

"Is that—?" he said, his eyes widening. He took the object from her and stared at the small digital screen on one side. It had a line running down the right-hand side and a much fainter one to the left. He looked to the key which was printed next to the display and stared at it. A single line meant you weren't pregnant, two lines meant you were. "Does this mean that—?" he said, looking at Laura as the lift doors closed again.

"I don't know!' she said, rolling her eyes. "Look at the bloody thing! I mean, is that two lines or not?!"

Brock stared at the screen again. The line on the left was so faint, it almost wasn't there when you stared directly at it. "I don't know." He shrugged. "So you're...?"

"Just a few days late, it could be nothing." She took the test from him, threw it in her handbag and wiped her eyes. "Come on, let's go and find out what's going on with this pole."

He watched her storm out of the lift in a daze before shaking his head and following her. He passed Roland Hale and David Davies, who were both standing by the foot of the totem pole and staring up at it.

"I'll be honest," Brock said as he caught up with his wife. "Leaving those two at the bottom of the thing means we could well come back to it burnt to the ground."

"It's this way," Laura said, turning left down one of the rows of displays and clearly not buying his attempt at lightening the mood.

"We'll get another test, then we'll know," he said.

"Yes, and then we'll know," she replied, the resignation in her voice telling him that she had already made her mind up about what the answer was going to be. "But for now, shall we try and find out why someone's put something into my exhibit?"

Brock said nothing but followed her down the aisle, his mind in a whirl.

Was this it? Were they finally going to be parents? His mind moved away from the growing excitement he could feel in his gut to darker thoughts. Here they were at what should have been a moment of excitement, and instead they were set on this grim errand. And it was grim, he was sure of that. No one goes to the trouble of cracking open an artefact like that and putting something inside it without the reason being very troubling.

Laura opened a heavy door in the wall and they stepped through into a cool, dark corridor. They turned left and descended a steep staircase lit by fluorescent strip lights.

"The guy actually works down here?" Brock said, trying to think of something to say in the circumstances.

"Yes, Sam." Laura's tone was curt.

"I know you've told me that before, I just never thought it would be so, well, grim."

"Don't say that in front of Frazer, he's likely to smack you one."

Brock pictured Frazer as they descended into another short corridor. He had only met him a few times, and always out of the context of the museum. Usually at some staff do, Christmas dinner or summer barbecue. The white-haired, softly spoken Scotsman didn't seem the type to throw punches, but Laura had sounded as though she'd meant it.

He wasn't sure why, but Brock had always disliked the man. There was something about Frazer's eyes that set Brock's teeth on edge.

Laura knocked on a door set into the wall on their left.

"Come in," a voice came from the room beyond.

Laura opened it and stepped through with Brock following her.

"Frazer? We need your help."

Frazer was standing facing them, his hands leaning on a small table to either side of the laptop in front of him. He was a spritely, impish face man in his sixties. Thin-rimmed spectacles rested over warm, sparkling blue eyes. A wild mop of white hair contrasted with his neat beard.

"What's wrong?" he said, standing up.

"We think there's something—" She paused and looked at Brock.

"We think there might be something in the totem pole," Brock took over. "We need to open it now. Have you got anything to pry it open, like a crowbar?"

"Aye, I have," Frazer said, moving around the desk. "And I'm glad to see you here, Sam—I've just noticed that someone tried to break in here last night."

"Break in?" Laura said. "Where? How?"

"I'll show you, it's where the crowbar is, anyway."

They followed him back into the corridor and along until he opened a door on the left wall. They entered a large room that extended into the distance along rows of metal shelving which reached up to the ceiling.

"So, this is the storeroom?" Brock said, looking around.

"Are you trying to impress me with your detective skills. Sam?" Frazer chuckled.

Laura laughed as well, apparently breaking her previous bad mood. For some reason, this annoyed Brock more than he had wanted it to.

On the far side of the room, they came to a double-doored fire escape that had a length of thick chain slung around its push-open bars.

"That doesn't look very safe for a fire escape," Brock grunted.

"I've just put it on now while I can sort the doors out," Frazer said as he bent down and unlocked the padlock securing the chain. "Someone tried to force the mechanism." He pushed the doors open and stepped out into an alleyway which ran along the back of the museum. "Look for yourself," he said, gesturing to the doors.

Brock and Laura moved closer and looked.

"Someone's tried to lever it open all right," Brock said, peering at it. He got up and looked up and down the alley. One way ended in a high stone wall, the other led back out to a side street. "You've got a security camera?" Brock said, pointing to a light-grey shape on the wall as it ended at the street.

"Aye, just one that points to the entrance to the street, but someone smashed it with a rock or something last night. I was just trying to look at the footage when you came in, but there's nothing there."

"You've got an alarm system, presumably?"

"It didn't go off. It's all triggered by motion sensors inside, so if they didn't get in?" He shrugged.

Brock nodded and then fell silent. He stared at the door thoughtfully for a few moments, before he jumped back into life.

"I need you to stay here a moment until I can get an officer down to secure the scene," he said.

"Will do. I was due a cigarette break anyway," Frazer answered, winking at Laura.

"Where's this crowbar?" Brock snapped.

"It's back the way we came, to the left of the door back into the hall. I use it to open crates down here sometimes."

Brock grunted and turned back into the storeroom.

"What time does he normally arrive?" Brock asked as Laura caught up with him, moving back down the metal aisle.

"Who, Frazer? I've no idea. He seems to practically live here, to be honest. Why?"

"I'm just wondering how long it took him to notice that

someone had tried to break in. I mean, it's six o'clock in the evening."

"Well, how was he supposed to know if the alarm didn't go off? This isn't the Natural History Museum in London, you know. We're not exactly hi-tech."

Brock said nothing and continued with his long stride, Laura hurrying to keep up beside him. They reached the door, and he walked along the wall to the left until he found the crowbar and they made their way back into the museum.

The large room was a different place than the one they had left. Suddenly the high glass panes above them reflected voices and the sound of glasses clinking.

Brock looked down at Laura beside him and saw the lines of concern etched on her face. What was she thinking about right now? Tonight's party? What was in that totem pole? Or whether their dream had become a reality, and she was pregnant?

As they reached the main avenue between the exhibits, they glanced back towards the entrance. Waiting staff were milling around and setting out the glasses and bubbly on white-clothed tables.

"The plan is to keep everyone up there for a while with the drinks and nibbles, then move everyone down to the pole at around seven," Laura said, guessing what Brock was thinking.

They turned back towards the pole where Hale and Davies were still standing. Hale was looking in through the glass of a display case, Davies standing to attention at the base of the pole. His head swivelled left and right, periodically looking for people to turn away from the area.

Brock said nothing to them as they passed, but headed straight for the lift where they rose in silence until the doors pinged open and they made their way to Poole and Sanita.

"Here we go then," Brock said as he hefted the crowbar. "You might want to stand back a bit," he said to the group. Laura scowled at him but moved back anyway.

He teased the prongs of the bar into the gap at the top of the panel where the wood had already been damaged and pulled downwards. There was a creak of wood as the panel gave way and fell out in front of them.

There, squashed into the recess of the mortuary pole, was a man. His lifeless eyes stared out at them, unseeing.

CHAPTER TWO

"What took you so long?" Poole said, taking a coffee from the tray Roland Hale was carrying.

"Davies spilt the first lot, and we had to clean it up and remake it," Hale replied bitterly.

"Sorry, sir," Davies said, looking sheepish. Sanita chuckled and shook her head, taking two cups from the tray and passing one to Poole.

"I'm just going to talk to the inspector," Poole said to Sanders in a hushed tone.

She looked across the aisle at the thunderous expression on Brock's face and nodded. "Good luck."

"How bloody long does it take to stop a party?" Brock muttered as Poole came alongside him.

He was staring down the aisle to where Laura and her colleagues were turning the confused guests away with free museum stickers and pens.

"About as long as it takes crime scene to get here on a Friday night, apparently," Poole said, sipping at his coffee.

Like the inspector, he was not in a good mood.

An hour ago he had arrived at the museum with Sanita, his mind full of happy thoughts for the first time in weeks. He finally had the flat to himself for once, as his mother had disappeared to a health spa with a friend for the week. This had given him the rare courage to invite Sanita back to his place.

In the weeks since he had plucked up the courage to ask her out, they had been on precisely three dates. Tonight was supposed to be the fourth.

Still, he thought, at least his mother was gone for a while. Things at his flat had been tense to say the least. Not that his mother seemed to have noticed. She knew something was wrong, but had no idea the source of the tension was Poole's discovery that she was the one who had been responsible for alerting the rival drug gang who had then shot him and killed his friend. Every time he looked at his mother, spoke to her, he felt the same rage and anguish he had with his father.

His friend had died that day all those years ago, and his father had been taken away from him because of it. It had been the end of one life and the start of another for him, but the old wounds kept reopening.

Now he faced another murder, and knew his time at home would be fleeting for the foreseeable future, and that he and Sanita would have to wait. Particularly as this crime had happened at the workplace of Laura Brock.

He looked at the inspector now. His eyes burning, his wide jaw tense. There was something about his demeanour that had Poole on edge. He seemed wired, angry. As though he was taking this personally. Whatever the reason, Poole would not want to be the person responsible. Being in jail might be safer.

"Do you think the break-in is related, sir?" Poole asked,

deciding that distracting the inspector from whatever was seething inside his mind was a good idea.

"It's a bloody coincidence, isn't it?" Brock said. "But Frazer says the doors were still closed when he got there and the alarm hadn't been set off, so I can't see how they would have got the body in."

"Unless they found another way when they couldn't get through the doors?" Poole said.

"Maybe. This old place isn't the most secure of buildings."

"Seems a bit odd having lax security at a museum," Poole said, aware that he might be treading on eggshells here with this being Laura's place of work.

"Despite it being a museum there's not a lot of real value you could get away with," Brock answered. "It's mostly odds and ends from all over the world, cultural stuff."

Brock had said these last two words as though he were describing a particularly nasty foot fungus.

"So why try to break in at all?" Poole shrugged. "It has to be something to do with it."

"It could be a coincidence, could have just been kids messing about. I guess we'll find out, won't we?" Brock grunted.

Poole turned back to the entrance in the distance and saw Sheila Hopkins and her crime scene assistants passing through the throng.

"What are we looking at?" Sheila said when she reached them. Her mousy brown hair twisted up on top of her head, she wore a rather dark and dramatic eyeshadow, and large hoop earrings which swayed as she came to a halt.

"A body in a totem pole, would you believe?" Brock said, turning and heading away from her. Sheila followed with Poole, her two assistants bringing up the rear.

"Sorry for disturbing your Friday night," Poole said.

"My Friday nights are no concern of yours, Sergeant," she replied with a smile, appearing glad that at least someone had noticed she was dressed up. "What's wrong with the inspector?"

"I think he's just got the hump because someone's left a dead body here on his wife's big night," Poole replied. Though he wasn't sure he believed that was all it was, he decided not to share this thought with Sheila. They reached the base of the totem pole and looked up at it.

"The compartment's at the top," Brock said as they joined him. "We opened it with a crowbar and, before you say anything," Brock said hurriedly, sensing Sheila was about to admonish him for disturbing the scene, "we didn't know what would be in there. For all we knew it could have been some old rags, or even someone alive."

"OK," Sheila said, looking up at the piece. "We'll sweep everything at the base in case they dropped any evidence, and then we'll move up to the top. Once we've checked the area, we'll need to lay it flat to do the rest."

Brock nodded. "I've already talked to Laura about that. They had some sort of specialist crane to put it up, she's going to call the company again when she gets rid of that lot. We'll need to speak to them, anyway."

"OK, we'll get on with it then," Sheila said and headed off to the two assistants who she barked out instructions to.

"What are you thinking, Poole?" Brock asked as they watched them set to their work.

Poole thought for a moment. He had always felt that when the inspector asked him what he thought of a case, he was testing him.

"I think there are probably only three options. The first is that someone here at the museum did it." He watched as the corner of Brock's mouth twitched into a smile. Poole knew the inspector would be happy he wouldn't rule Laura out just because she was married to the boss. "The second is that whoever tried to break into the storeroom last night found some other way in. Then they either killed their accomplice or decided to dump the body here."

"And the third?" Brock asked, one eyebrow rising as it always did when he asked a question he was particularly interested in.

"Well, I think the third is the most likely to be honest, sir. I mean, if you killed someone in here there are loads of places you could hide a body—it's full of cabinets and things. I can't see someone thinking to prise open the hatch on the totem pole and do it."

"And so the most likely option is...?" Brock pressed.

"That someone put the body into the totem pole after Laura and her team did the ultrasound, but before it was transported to the museum."

"Which leads us to the manor house," Brock said, nodding. "We need to get over there sharpish, but I want to talk to Laura and the rest of the people here first."

"Yes, sir," Poole said as they turned back down the main aisle. There was something in the way the inspector had spoken his wife's name, something hard in his voice. Poole wondered for a moment if the inspector actually suspected she had something to do with this, but quickly put the thought out of his mind.

CHAPTER THREE

Twenty minutes later, Brock and Poole were sitting at a meeting table in the main office of the museum. Opposite them sat the remaining staff: Laura, Frazer Mullins and Jemima Shaw.

After giving them details and an overview of their movements, the catering staff had been sent home. Nancy Cole had been sent home too. She was visibly shaken by a dead body in the museum, and as it had been determined that she didn't have a key to the building or the code for the alarm, she had been allowed to leave with her father, who had come to pick her up.

"So, the totem pole arrived yesterday?" Brock said as Poole scribbled in his notepad next to him. The other three were sitting opposite them, which seemed strange with Laura being one of the group. The office they were sitting in was a large square. Lining the walls were posters of various artefacts that Poole was sure were too grand to be found in this museum. The room contained two desks against the far wall, as well as the meeting table. Poole had no trouble spotting which desk belonged to Laura, with its framed picture of Brock and their dog Indy standing proudly to one side of the workspace.

"Yes," Jemima answered. "It arrived on a truck and was brought in using some mobile winch thing. A company handled it all, Holt Handling, they specialise in this sort of stuff."

"And they moved it into position?"

"Yes."

Poole appraised Jemima Shaw for a moment. Her dark blue eyes were set above high cheekbones. She had an air of wealth about her, as well as poise and class.

"And no one inspected the pole once it was here?" Brock continued.

"No, there didn't seem any need to. We'd looked it over at the manor house and got an expert across from Oxford to do the ultrasound and things. There wasn't much else to look over."

The inspector took a deep breath. "We'll need this expert's details as well, but tell me about this manor house. What's the setup?"

"It's owned by the Pentonvilles, been in the family for centuries. The place is big enough that it costs a fortune to run, but too small to make much of a tourist attraction."

"The family coffers are running low?" Brock asked.

Jemima laughed. "I don't think so. William Pentonville was apparently loaded. Inherited an absolute fortune from his father, who was also responsible for the mortuary pole." She looked up, saw Brock's questioning eyes and continued. "His father was a well-travelled man and liked to collect objects from the places he visited. It's rumoured there's a very valuable collection spread around the manor house and its grounds."

"Then why did William Pentonville only leave the totem pole to the museum?"

"No idea," Jemima said, shrugging. "All I know is his sons didn't seem very happy about it."

"Oh?"

"I tried to talk to them about allowing us to look at some of their other pieces on the grounds. That their father may have intended to bequest more to the museum, but simply didn't know what he had."

"And I take it they weren't on board with this idea?"

"You could say that." Jemima laughed, turning to Laura.

"Both of them are money-grabbing creeps," Laura said vehemently. "Simon and Clive Pentonville, they're called. They made it pretty clear to us that the first thing they were going to do was to sell everything off to the highest bidder and sod the family heritage."

Poole watched Jemima shift uncomfortably. He wondered if it was due to Laura's bluntness rather than the rather cheap office chair she was sitting on.

"And presumably this totem pole is valuable?" Brock asked.

"Not particularly," Laura answered. "It's a much smaller market for pieces like this. They usually go to heritage centres or museums in the area that the object is from. There's virtually no private market for it, like some of the smaller objects we've got here."

"But you were planning on keeping it here?"

"Yes," Laura answered.

"Excuse me, Inspector," Jemima said suddenly, "but could we continue this tomorrow? It's been a long day and I'm wondering when I can go home?"

"Our people will be here most of the night, maybe all of

it, but we'll need someone to lock up once everything's been checked over," Brock answered

"Don't worry about that," Frazer said in his light Scottish tone. "I don't have anywhere to be, and as long as I've got coffee and some baccy I'll be grand."

"Thanks, Frazer," Jemima said, rising. "That OK with you, Inspector?"

"Fine," Brock grumbled, his eyes now locked on Laura, who had also risen.

"Jemima's going to drop me at home, Sam," she said, looking awkward.

"Can I have a word before you go?" Brock said quietly.

Poole watched the two of them as they headed through the door of the office after Jemima. Something was going on there. Maybe an argument?

"Looks like trouble in paradise to me, eh?" Frazer said, his eyes alive with mischief.

Poole got up and stared back at him. "A man has been found dead tonight, Mr Mullins. I don't think it's the time for gossiping about a colleague's love life, do you?"

Frazer's smile faded as Poole turned and left the room.

Back in the large main room of the museum, he could see the inspector and Laura talking in a hushed tone. He waited, his eyes scanning the magnificent ceiling until they parted. There was a brief peck on the cheek before Laura Brock followed Jemima, who had been waiting by the entrance, down the main stairs and out of sight.

"Everything OK, sir?" Poole said as Brock lumbered over.

"Fine," he replied, in a tone that suggested it was anything but. "I think we should pay a little visit to the manor house, find out exactly where this pole was kept and who had access to it."

"Yes, sir," Poole replied, concerned about his two friends.

CHAPTER FOUR

"Bloody hell, how long is this driveway?" Brock said as he fished in his pocket.

They were driving along a small, sloping road that wound its way through bright green grass. Before long, they saw Otworth Manor looming against the darkening skyline.

Brock finally found what he had been looking for and produced a battered packet of cigarettes.

"Sir?" Poole said, glancing at them surprised. He had expected the normal packet of boiled sweets to emerge.

"Tonight is not the night for you to play the angel on my shoulder telling me what I should and shouldn't do, Poole."

The low and flat way he had said this sent a slight shiver down Poole's spine, and he decided not to mention the cigarettes again.

Which he didn't, not even when Brock wound the creaking window of the Ford Mondeo down and lit it. Instead, Poole wound his window down as well and leaned towards it.

They pulled onto a gravelled portion of the drive that

skirted a neatly trimmed circle of grass. The building itself was built from a dark grey stone, in contrast to the butter-yellow stone that made up the buildings of Bexford. Two large wings jutted forward, creating a mini-courtyard in front of the entrance, which was set back into the main part of the building. Dim light filtered through the tall windows at various places, and several cars were parked in the drive.

"Someone's home at least," Brock grunted as he climbed out of the car, allowing its suspension to wheeze a sigh of relief.

"Are Range Rovers the only cars available around here, sir?" Poole asked, gesturing to the three identical vehicles which were only separated by either their colour or the amount of mud on them.

"Gives them all the luxury of a fancy car while still feeling like they're being Lord and Lady Muck in the countryside," Brock muttered.

As they climbed the four worn steps to the front door, the sound of laughter and voices filtered through the thin windows on either side.

"Sounds like someone's having a party," Poole said as he pressed the doorbell.

Brock grunted but said nothing, instead stubbing his cigarette out on the wall. Poole watched him take the packet out from his jacket and place the cigarette butt in it and smiled to himself. The inspector hated littering.

After a few moments, the door opened to reveal a man in his mid-thirties wearing a pale blue shirt with one too many buttons undone. He held a large glass of red wine in his left hand and his mop of black hair was looking slightly dishevelled.

"Can I help you?" he said with a frown of suspicion.

"I'm Detective Inspector Brock and this is Detective Sergeant Poole. Can I ask who you are?"

"What do you want?" the man replied before taking a slug of wine.

"Right now?" Brock asked as he took a step forward. "Right now, I'd like to know who the bloody hell you are."

"I'm Simon Pentonville and this is my house, so I think I'm bloody entitled to ask what the hell you're doing here?" Although the man had delivered this with a fair amount of vigour, Poole couldn't help but notice there was a hint of a smile at the corner of his lips. As though he enjoyed being the outraged landowner.

"Who is it, Simon?" a female voice called out from behind him. "Tell them to bugger off unless they've got any more cigarettes, I'm almost out!"

Simon's lip curled into a smile. "It's the police, Ellie, I think they've come to arrest us all for having a good time."

"No, actually, Mr Pentonville, we've come to find out whether a murder was committed on this property in the last few days," Brock said, his jaw clenched.

Poole started mentally preparing a witness statement for when Brock walloped this drunken idiot.

"A murder?!" a female voice screeched from behind Simon Pentonville. The woman, blonde-haired and wearing a gold-coloured wrap over a purple cocktail dress, fell onto the man's shoulder and grinned at them. "How exciting! Who's been murdered?"

"No one's been bloody murdered," Simon said, laughing. "This must be some kind of joke!"

"It's no joke, Mr Pentonville. A man was found murdered in the totem pole that your father left to Bexford Museum in his will."

Simon Pentonville's face hardened. He straightened up, suddenly looking soberer. "What are you talking about?"

"Could we come in please, sir?" Poole said, attempting to diffuse for a moment what he could see was a rising tension.

Simon pushed the door open and turned down the large hallway with his arm around Ellie's waist.

The hallway itself was dominated by a large central staircase which rose upwards in front of them before splitting off left and right. A few pieces of old and heavy-looking wooden furniture were dotted around the walls, as were some landscapes, which hung in ornate frames. They looked as though they had been there for centuries.

"Go and tell the others I'll just be a moment," he said to her. She rolled her eyes and headed through a door on the left. Simon gestured for Brock and Poole to follow him through a door on the opposite side of the hall.

They entered a large study whose walls were lined with shelves full of small and bizarre objects. Statues, ceremonial knives, tapestries set in frames, and even what looked like a small collection of voodoo dolls.

A large, oak desk was to their left, and Simon Pentonville sat behind it in a leather swivel chair. Brock and Poole took the two leather seats in front of the desk, with Poole pulling his notebook from his pocket.

"What the hell do you mean there was a body in the bloody totem pole?" Simon said, his whole demeanour suddenly very different from the cocky drunk they had met at the door.

"At approximately seven pm this evening the compartment at the back of the mortuary pole was opened and a man's body was discovered."

"But that's impossible," Simon countered. "They came

and scanned the thing, there was nothing in it." He sounded more hopeful than incredulous.

"Well, believe me, Mr Pentonville, there was something in it when we opened it earlier this evening. Where was the totem pole stored when it was here?"

"In the barn down by the stables. That's where the museum people did their test, and then a truck turned up and took it away the next day."

"And is the barn secure?"

"Of course it's secure! There's a padlock on the doors."

"And who would have a key to that padlock?" Brock continued. Poole noticed he seemed to have calmed down now he was in the groove of questioning.

"Only me, my brother, Lucy, and Ted."

"Your brother would be Clive Pentonville, would he?"

"Yes." Simon leaned forward and took another long slug of his wine.

"And where is he at the moment?"

"In London on business."

"And who are Ted and Lucy?"

"Ted's the estate manager, but he's an odd-job man really, and Lucy manages the business."

"What business is that?"

"The stables, other people keep their horses here and pay stable fees."

"Has anyone been in the barn since the museum came to run the scan on the compartment?"

"God knows, I'm not exactly down there keeping an eye on the place. You'll have to talk to Lucy or Ted."

"You'd better go and find us their contact details then, hadn't you?" Brock said.

Simon gave a grunt of annoyance and pulled a drawer in

the desk out, producing a small black book. He opened it to where a red ribbon kept the page and slid it over to them.

"There you go. Now can you leave me and my friends in peace?"

"Who exactly is here tonight?" Brock asked.

"None of your business," Simon replied before finishing his wine. "You can show yourself out."

He rose and moved around the desk only to walk straight into the chest of Brock, who had also risen.

"Do you know what exactly constitutes 'my business' when there's a murder inquiry, Mr Pentonville?" the inspector said, looking down at Simon as though he was a bug to be squashed. "Everything. And that includes your little get-together here, OK?"

Simon Pentonville swore as he ducked past him and back out into the hall.

Brock took a deep breath and gestured for Poole to go first. They stepped through the door, and across the hall where Simon had left the door open. His voice spilt out as they approached, telling his friends about their intrusion.

"And they seem to think the body was stuffed in the bloody thing before it left here," he said as they passed into the room.

The group turned to the doorway as they entered.

"And here they are," Ellie said, raising a glass of something bubbly. "Addervale's finest, here to find themselves a murderer!"

"Good evening, ladies and gentlemen," Brock said, ignoring her. "We need your names, addresses and whereabouts over the last few days."

"Not one for small talk, is he?" Ellie said before roaring with laughter. The others smiled, but didn't laugh with her. There were four of them, including Simon Pentonville.

Ellie leaned back in a chair on the far side of the long oval dinner table with an amused smile on her face. A woman on the right of her shared Ellie's amused expression, but it was coupled with intelligent eyes and delicate features.

There was a man opposite her, to the left of Ellie. He leaned back, one arm on the back of his chair, and seemed relaxed. He was good-looking, with deep brown eyes that sparkled in the light from the chandelier which hung above the table.

There were remnants of a dinner on the table, but these had been pushed to the middle to make way for bottles of wine and spirits which now dominated the space in front of the guests.

"Can I ask each of you to state your name, please?" Brock said, his grey eyes scanning the room slowly.

"Oh!" Ellie said, "it's like Alcoholics Anonymous, but for murder suspects, isn't it?! OK, I'll go first." She got up, put her hands together in front of her and bowed her head. "My name is Ellie Kendall and I'm a murder suspect." She snorted with laughter and was joined by the others in the room as she fell back into a chair in a fit of giggles.

Brock said nothing but folded his arms and stared. Gradually the room quietened, and the woman with the mousy hair spoke.

"I'm Helen Blaxon," she said coolly, her dark eyes fixed on the inspector's. "And this is Jonathan Finley," she said, gesturing to the man opposite her.

"Oh Helen," Ellie whined. "You've killed all our fun!"

"Let's hope that's the only thing she's killed, eh?" Jonathan said, causing another burst of laughter from Ellie.

"How long have you all been here tonight?" Brock said, his loud voice cutting through the laughter.

"We've been here all week, Mr Policeman!" Ellie said, giggling.

"You've all been staying at the house here?"

"Yes, look, is that all?" Simon said, speaking for the first time since he had re-entered the room. "I don't see what good all this is doing at this time of night. If you really must speak to us, can't you come back tomorrow?"

"I'm going to have to get a couple of officers to come and guard the barn until morning, when I can get a crime scene unit over here."

"Do whatever you like down there, I don't care."

Brock nodded at Poole, and they turned towards the door. As soon as they stepped out into the hall, they heard voices and a roar of laughter from behind them.

"We're not going to get much out of that lot tonight," Brock grumbled. They paused by the door as he checked his watch. "It's getting too late to do much of anything now. We'll have a quick look at the barn and then get a couple of officers here. We can call on the other two with keys in the morning, or they might even turn up here."

"Yes, sir." Poole stepped out into the cool night and looked up. Although they were only ten miles from Bexford, the night sky was noticeably fuller. Stars seemed to fill the blackness as though someone had scattered snow across a black sheet above them.

"Where are these stables then, sir? Simon said the barn's by them, didn't he?" Poole said, looking around the small courtyard at the front of the house.

"I didn't see them on the way in, so they must be at the back."

They headed around the large house, using a small path which ran along a flower bed that looked as though it had once been impressive, but now needed weeding.

The lawn at the back of the house sloped down a small hill, at the bottom of which some buildings were just visible in the dim light from the moon which skated behind the thin clouds above.

They descended in silence, except for the occasional grunt from Brock, whose fitness left something to be desired.

As the slope flattened, the ground turned into fine red gravel that covered a wide, flat area in front of the buildings. There were stables in rows; one to the left, one to the right. In between them at the back was a building designed in a similar style to the stables, but instead of the large sliding doors, this one was fronted with glass.

"Looks like an office of some kind, sir," Poole said as they approached. The telltale red lights of a computer and router were visible through the glass, and the shape of a desk set against the window could just be made out.

"I think our destination's back there, don't you?" Brock said, pointing to the right of the building. Through the gap between the right-hand stable and the office block was the large, hulking shape of a barn.

They headed through the gap and walked across to the large metal sliding doors.

"Well the padlock's still here," Poole said, lifting the thick silver lock. "And it doesn't look damaged."

"Have a walk around it, will you?" Brock said, standing back and looking up at the structure. "See if there's any other way in."

Poole headed off down the side of the barn, which was far bigger than he had thought from the front. Although quite low in height it was long, its corrugated metal side stretching out into the dark in front of him. He pulled his phone from his pocket and switched on the torch application.

He had made his way around the bulk of the building

without seeing anything of note when, just as he approached the front end of the building where Brock was standing, something caught his eye. There was a track here, leading off to his right and across a field into the darkness. At its edge, something gave off a dull reflection of the moonlight. Poole approached and bent down to the object.

"What is it, Poole?" Brock called, approaching from behind.

"A crowbar, sir."

CHAPTER FIVE

Poole closed the door of his flat behind him and moved straight to the fridge where he pulled out a beer and cracked it open before flopping onto the sofa.

The place felt quiet and strange without his mother here. She'd moved in so soon after he did that there had barely been a time when he had been here alone.

He felt the now all-too-familiar pang deep in his gut. It had been just over three weeks since he'd discovered the truth about the incident from his childhood that had put a bullet in his thigh. He hadn't heard from his father since he'd told Poole this revelation. More importantly, he hadn't yet worked up the courage to say anything to his mum.

She knew something was wrong, though, and he half suspected that this spa trip was to get away from him for a few days. Why hadn't he told her? Was it because he didn't want to face the fact that his mother might be just as responsible for the incident as his father? Or was it that he wasn't sure how she would react?

He knew it was only a matter of time: he couldn't live like

this for much longer. At some point he would have to face the truth, and so would his mother.

His phone buzzed in his pocket and he immediately thought it would be her messaging to check in from her spa. Instead, it was Sanita's name that appeared on the screen.

"Sorry about tonight, let's rain-check until all the murders are out of the way! X"

He smiled as he felt the familiar warm glow that always seemed to appear whenever he talked to Sanita, or even just looked at her. He read the message again, and this time with a sinking feeling.

He hadn't yet told her about his past, about what had happened to his family and his friends. He wasn't looking forward to telling her about the problems it was still causing, the distance between himself and his parents, the nightmares he still had.

"Until all the murders were out of the way," she had said. Would they ever be? Would the murder from his own past ever be out of the way?

He took another long slug of cold beer, lay back and closed his eyes.

CHAPTER SIX

"I've left your dinner in the fridge, you just need to heat it up," Laura called from the front room, as Brock kicked his shoes off in the hall.

"Thanks," he shouted back.

The familiar scurrying of claws on wood made him look up. Indy was scrambling towards him, his body bending left and right with the sheer force of his tail wagging.

"Hello boy," Brock said, bending to stroke the dog. He got up and took a deep breath, trying to ready himself for another disappointment. Ready to console Laura yet again as their dream of having a child was snatched away. He had to make sure he was there for her; he'd deal with his own feelings later.

He stepped into the living room and saw Laura look up at him. She was sitting cross-legged on the sofa, staring at a small box on the coffee table in front of her.

"Well? What does it say?" he said, moving over to peer down at the pregnancy test.

"I don't know, I haven't looked yet."

"Haven't looked? But you've done the test?"

"Yes, I've done it. I just haven't looked yet." Laura's voice was strange, distant somehow. Her eyes hadn't left the box.

"OK," Brock said, sitting down next to her. "We'll look at it together." He took her right hand in his left and reached forward to pick up the box with his right. He placed it on his knee and reached in to pull the thin device out and held it in front of them.

They stared at it in silence for what felt like hours but Brock knew was only a few moments. "Laura, are those two lines?" he said, his voice catching in his suddenly tight throat.

"Oh my God! Sam!" Laura screamed, tears already rolling down her cheeks. She turned to him and hugged him tightly as she fell into heavy sobs.

"Bloody hell," Brock said quietly in her ear. "We're having a baby."

She started to laugh as she pulled away from him, falling backwards in uncontrollable hysterical giggling.

Brock laughed too, staring at the indicator still in his hand.

Laura managed to control herself enough to point at it. "That's the end I weed on!" she said before falling back in laughter again.

Brock was laughing hard now, falling back on the sofa and feeling the sting of tears as he and his wife bathed in the pure joy of the moment.

CHAPTER SEVEN

Poole stared at the inspector. Brock was sitting opposite him, tucking into a double helping of pretty much every fried food the canteen at Bexford Police Station had to offer. Something was definitely off with Brock this morning.

Not only had he been beaming for the past twenty minutes, he had also ordered this breakfast unashamedly. There was no hint of guilt or concern that Poole might inform his wife of the indiscretion.

"Sounds like there are no prints on the crowbar we found," Poole said, wondering if this bad news would burst Brock's bubble somewhat.

"Didn't think there would be," the inspector replied cheerily. "People watch enough crime programs on TV to know to wear gloves or wipe the thing down."

"It looks like the one used to open the totem pole, though," Poole continued. "The marks match up to the prongs at the end, and bearing in mind where we found it."

"The thing is," Brock said, placing his cutlery down on

his plate and leaning back satisfied, "the crowbar doesn't actually make sense."

"How do you mean?" Poole asked.

"Well, say the killer had already murdered this chap, and they have him in a car. Why drive all the way along that back road into the estate, get into the barn somehow, break open the compartment, and then put the body in there? They could have dumped them anywhere."

"Then they must have killed him in the barn?"

"Aha!" Brock said, grinning.

This jovial attitude was really unnerving Poole.

"That's the problem with the crowbar," Brock expanded. "Let's say they killed him there; where did they get the crowbar from?"

"Maybe it was in the barn already?"

"Exactly what I thought, but then why would you leave it outside after you'd used it to get into the pole and stuff a body in there? You'd leave it where you found it, wouldn't you? So as not to draw attention to it?"

"Yes," Poole said slowly. Brock was right, it didn't really make sense to find the crowbar where they did.

"So why was it there?"

"Well," said Brock, still smiling broadly. "It occurred to me that you wouldn't need the crowbar to shut the compartment, only to open it."

Poole frowned. "I'm sorry, but I don't see what difference that makes?"

"Neither do I yet, but it's a thought, isn't it? Come on, let's go and talk to the other owners of the keys, this Ted Daley and Lucy Flowers. They're both on their way to the manor so we should be too, but I want to see if we've got an ID on our body first." He got up, paused, and looked down at

Poole, who hadn't moved. He was staring at him in an odd way, a deep frown across his forehead.

"Is everything OK, sir?" Poole asked.

"Fine, Poole! Absolutely fine!" The inspector turned and headed for the door.

Poole rose and followed in a thoughtful mood.

CHAPTER EIGHT

"Well, you do keep turning up bodies in the most unusual places, don't you, Sam?" Ronald Smith said, his beady little eyes gleaming. "I mean to say, a totem pole!"

"What have you got for us, Ron?" Brock said, his good mood visibly fraying at the edges in the presence of the pathologist.

"I mean, people are going to start talking if you keep turning them up like this," Ronald continued, unable to pass up an opportunity to wind up another human being.

"Listen, Ron," Brock said, his voice hard. "I don't think you're in a position to be talking to us about being on the scene when a body is discovered, do you? It was only a couple of weeks ago you were a suspect in a murder inquiry, one which we helped you out of."

Ronald gave a weak smile and cleared his throat before looking down at the folder in front of him. "The man was approximately thirty-two years old, in fairly good health.

Killed by a blow to the back of the head. I doubt he knew much about it. He's not in the system I'm afraid, so until you can get some more information to me, we're not going to know who he is."

"When did he die?" Brock asked.

"It's hard to tell as we don't know where or when he entered the totem pole. The space was fairly well sealed which would have kept the bugs out, and if he was in the barn at the manor house for some time, then that would change things as I'd imagine it's colder. I'd say sometime between Tuesday and Thursday."

Brock sighed. "Helpful as ever, Ron," he said as he rose from his seat.

"There is one thing I thought you'd find interesting," Ronald said, his tone teasing.

Brock paused, his hand on the office door. "What is it?"

"Whoever this man is, I believe he had money and that he may not have earned it through legal means."

"Oh? Why do you say that?" Brock said as he turned slowly back into the small office.

"Well, he'd had expensive dental work, hair plugs. Looks like he'd even had some minor plastic surgery."

"That points to money, what about the criminal element?"

"The man has a few scars around his body, but in particular, there is a nasty one on his abdomen, which I believe was caused by a knife. Now, of course, this could have been a domestic incident, but together with the money it does make you wonder."

Poole felt his ears grow hot as he thought of the bullet scar on his leg.

"Good work, Ron," Brock said before opening the door and heading out of it.

"My, my, did I just hear some praise?" Ronald said to Poole, who was also moving for the door.

"Maybe you'd hear it more often if you were always that helpful," Poole said grumpily, leaving before the little man could reply.

CHAPTER NINE

"And you both have your keys on you?" Brock said, looking at the two people before him.

Lucy Flowers was a plump, middle-aged woman with hard eyes. Her grey-flecked brown hair was tied back in a practical bun, and she wore a blue skirt and jacket that gave her a headmistress look.

Ted Daley, who was standing next to her, was a long-limbed man of a similar age. He wore a flat cap and a wax jacket that looked as though he had worn it so long it had moulded to his body. His skin had the leathery look of a man who spent much of his life outdoors.

They both nodded and fished in their pockets to produce the keys.

"And these keys haven't been out of your sight in the last few days?"

"Never," Ted replied.

"Of course not," Lucy replied. "Look, Mr... Brock, was it? I can assure you that this barn has remained locked and as there are no signs of forced entry, I think we can assume that whoever this poor unfortunate person is, they were put into that ghastly pole after it had left here."

"Thank you for your insight, Mrs Flowers," Brock said, smiling. "Can we have a moment to talk to you first?"

"Of course," Lucy Flowers answered.

Brock turned to Ted Daley. "And then we will come and find you, Mr Daley."

"All right," Daley said, turning and loping off towards the stables.

"So, Mrs Flowers, can you tell me nothing you think might be of interest from the last week? Anything unusual occurred? Anyone new around the place?"

"Ha!' she said, folding her arms. "I could give you a list of new, unsavoury characters around here straight away!"

Brock said nothing but raised an eyebrow.

"Since William died, I'm afraid the place has been overrun by Simon and his little gang."

"You mean the guests staying up at the house?" Poole asked.

"Guests? More like parasites. The moment William died they descended, walking around the place as if they own it and declaring what they would get rid of if they were in charge."

There was something in the way she had said this and trailed off that prompted Brock to push the point. "And had they suggested getting rid of you, Mrs Flowers?"

She looked up, her cheeks reddening. "These stables have been here for years. William built up the business himself before handing it over to me, but those two don't give a damn about their father or what he wanted."

"And has Clive Pentonville been here with their guests this week as well?"

"No, Clive went to London midweek."

"And you have a key to the barn, don't you? Can you tell us why?"

"We store some of the stable's gear in there. It's a big space and only the back half is filled with junk."

"It can't all be junk, though? I mean, the totem pole that's gone to the museum is apparently quite a piece," Brock said. "There might be some things of value in there."

"I wouldn't know, Inspector," Lucy said quickly. "I'm in the horse business, not antiques."

"We're going to need to take that key, and we'll be in touch again shortly," Brock said, holding his hand out.

Lucy Flowers placed the key in his hand and turned away towards the stables.

"There's something about her I don't like," Brock said as they watched her leave.

"If we suspected everyone you didn't like, sir, I think our suspect pool would be too large to get anywhere."

Brock raised an eyebrow at him.

"Sorry, sir," Poole said, trying to control his grin.

"Is there still no word from tracking down the brother in London?" Brock asked.

"No, sir," Poole replied. He thought for a moment and turned to the inspector. "Do you think he's the victim, sir?"

"I think we might need to get Simon Pentonville in for an ID," the inspector answered. "Come on; let's speak to this Ted chap."

They headed across to the stables where Ted Daley was talking to a young man who was leading a large brown mare out of a stall. He saw them approach and moved to meet them.

"I haven't been in that barn for a month or so," he said as

they reached him. "Never had need to. I've got a work shed towards the back gate that all my stuff's in."

"Why do you have a key, then?" Brock asked bluntly.

"Because I'm the one they call if they want something moving or fixing. I've got a key to everything on the estate."

"You must know this place better than anyone," Brock said, folding his arms. "Tell us about the place."

Ted's mouth squirmed as though he was chewing on something. "Don't know what there is to tell," he said, shrugging. "I came to work for William when I was just a lad. I lived in the village, and he took me on as a gardener. Over time I came to just doing whatever he needed sorting around the place."

"What was he like, William Pentonville?" Poole asked.

Ted's face spread into a broad smile. "He was from the old school; they don't make them like that anymore. He was a gent, just like his father. Knew the land and knew the locals by name. He didn't lord things over like some." His face had darkened as he had spoken these last words, and Poole took the cue.

"You mean like his sons?"

"Yes," Ted said, looking him straight in the eye, his chin raised, "I do, and I don't care if they do bloody fire me. They don't deserve all this, never did, and William knew it too."

"What do you mean by that?" Brock asked.

"I mean William had told me that those lads were going to have a bit of a surprise when he passed, though I have to say I was expecting there to be more to it than what happened."

"What did happen?"

"Well, he left the two of them the house and the grounds to do whatever they wanted with. After what he'd said, I didn't think he'd do that."

"And what about the totem pole?"

Ted grinned. "Well, he left that to me! No idea why, daft sod."

"I'm sorry," Poole said, looking at the inspector and then back to Ted Daley. "You inherited the totem pole? We thought it had been left to the museum?"

"Well, it had in a way. He left me a note that said he knew I would do the right thing with it. It's not like it's going to fit in my little cottage garden and I wouldn't want it there, anyway. I guessed he meant to give it to a museum or something, so I did."

"Aren't there other artefacts here that might have been more valuable?"

"I wouldn't know about what's valuable and what isn't, but there's a tonne of stuff in that barn that William's father brought back from his travels. I dare say some, it must be worth something."

"So why the totem pole? What's special about it?"

"No idea. I was as surprised as anyone when I heard what he'd left me." His mouth began to writhe again. "To tell you the truth, I was hoping he'd leave me a little bit more. I rent the lodge over by the rear gate and I hoped he'd leave it to me, but there you go."

"And he didn't leave you any money or anything?"

"Nothing," Ted said, the disappointment in his voice obvious. "I'm in the hands of those two toe rags now, and Lord knows what they're going to do. Turn the place into some spa retreat or something."

"The brothers plan to turn the manor into a spa?" Poole asked, surprised.

"That's just what they were talking about last week; who knows what ideas they've got cooked up this week. All they really want to do is sell the place, but they don't think they're going to get much as it is."

"And why's that?" Brock asked. "Is the stable business not doing well?" He turned and looked back along the stalls where more horses were being led out and attached to the long fence pole which ran down the centre of the space.

"It's doing well enough, but William only liked it as a little thing to pay our wages and the upkeep of the place. Those two have bigger plans than that," he said, sighing as he looked up beyond the stables to the house on the hill behind.

"I think that's all for now," Brock said, his eyes resting on Constable Sanders who was making her way down from the house.

Ted loped off as Sanders arrived.

"Any news from our party at the house?" Brock asked, looking up at the place as Ted had done.

"Nope, they're all still in bed," she said, shaking her head. "The door was open when we went up there, so we went in and started shouting about and got told to sod off and come back later."

"Who by? Simon Pentonville?"

"I guess so, just a voice from upstairs. Heard a door slam again and so waited. Davies is still up there, I just wanted to know if you want me to make them get up?"

"No," Brock answered, his eyes narrowing. "I think we'll go and have a look in this barn first. You go back up and call me if they surface."

Brock turned back to the barn as Poole and Sanita hesitated, smiling awkwardly at each other.

"Sorry about last night," Poole said, breaking the silence.

"Don't worry, we've got all the time in the world." Sanita smiled back.

Poole forced a smile and turned away after Brock.

His stomach writhed with the familiar feeling of guilt and concern. They had all the time in the world. Time enough for Sanita to learn about his father's past, his mother's mistake. Time enough for her to become embroiled in the same awful mess he felt he was in.

CHAPTER TEN

B rock unclipped the padlock using Ted Daley's key and pulled one of the large doors sideways on its slide as Poole pulled the other.

Light flooded into the space as dust particles danced in the air and filtered out from inside. Poole moved in through the doors and found a large light switch to the right. He flicked it on and two rows of strip lights lit up along the high ceiling.

"Right, let's see what we've got, shall we?" Brock said.

The floor was rough concrete and covered in a fine layer of dust. The front end of the barn was clearly the storage area for the stables. Hay bales were stacked high against the left-hand wall, and on the right, various pieces of metal and leather hung in the dim light.

"Well, this is obviously the stable's storage area," Poole said, looking around.

"And I'm guessing the grandfather's collection from his travels is down there," Brock said, pointing.

Towards the back of the barn were rows of metal shelves,

around six feet in height, which stretched off into the distance.

They headed towards them and entered the row directly in front of them. On either side were various boxes and crates, each with a small handwritten label attached by a piece of string.

"Looks like the man was methodical, all of this is labelled up," Brock said.

"I'm surprised Laura wasn't pushing to get all of this stuff over to the museum," Poole said.

"She was," Brock replied in a grunt. "The two sons were having none of it."

They paused as they came to the end of the row. There was a gap here before the next rows started and as they looked left, they could see that it ran along the length of the barn.

"So where was the totem pole?" Brock said, frowning. "I mean, they couldn't fit it down one of these rows."

"It looks like there's a gap to the right-hand side, sir," Poole said, pointing.

They headed down the small avenue until they reached the right-hand wall of the barn. There was a large space between the end of the last row and the wall, and on the floor a long section of concrete that had a different shade to the rest.

"It looks like it was kept here," Brock said, crouching down by the void and looking up along its length. "We need Sheila to dust the walls for prints; they might have leaned on the wall when they were putting the body in." He got up and turned to Poole. "So? What do you think?"

Poole thought for a moment and looked back towards the open door. "If you just start with this place, then only a few things could have happened. Either one of the three who had a key—Simon Pentonville, Lucy Flowers or Ted Daley—opened this barn and stuffed the body in, or one of them opened it and left it unlocked."

"That wouldn't explain how it got locked up again," Brock interjected.

Poole shrugged. "Maybe they noticed later and locked it without realising anyone had been in there? Or maybe someone took one of the keys from them and then replaced it before it was missing?"

They both waited in silence for a moment, staring at the floor where the totem pole had lain and imagining the poor soul who had spent their last moments here.

"Right," Brock said, clapping his hands together. "Let's go and wake the lazy sods at the house up. I think it's time we got an ID on this body."

CHAPTER ELEVEN

Constables Sanders and Davies were standing in the hallway of the manor house with bored expressions.

"Still no sign of them?" Poole asked as he and Brock jogged up the steps to the wide-open doors.

"Oh, they're up," Sanita said. "They've gone in for breakfast, in a right state the lot of them. I'd be surprised if there's any booze left in the place, the way they look this morning."

"Then I'll remember to talk particularly loudly," Brock said with a malicious grin.

They moved down the hall and towards the door on the left that they had entered the previous night when Brock paused. He reached down and picked up a photograph that showed an older man and two young men, one of whom was Simon Pentonville, the other a blonde man who looked a little older, but nothing like the body they had pulled from the totem pole.

"Clive Pentonville," Brock said. "Doesn't look like our man in the totem pole to me."

Poole nodded, and they continued through the door.

"Good morning," Brock boomed as they entered. The people gathered around the table winced and Poole noticed a smile play on the inspector's lips.

"Bloody hell, man," Simon Pentonville said from the seat nearest them around the table. "Can you not let us get through breakfast before you come in here and start barking?"

"Mr Pentonville, I'm afraid I'm going to keep bothering you until we've got to the bottom of this. Now the first thing I want from you is a number or address where I can reach your brother in London."

"I don't bloody know where he is, I've already told you that," Simon said as he picked up a peppermill and ground it furiously over the scrambled eggs in front of him. "What Clive does is no concern of mine."

"Are the two of you not close?"

There was a general murmur of amusement from around the table.

"It's a wonder they haven't killed each other before now!" Ellie Kendall brayed before she suddenly clamped her hand over her mouth. "Oh, Lord! I didn't mean that!"

"We need to speak to each of you individually, it shouldn't take long," Brock said cheerily.

"Look," Simon said, turning to him. "I don't know how that bloody chap got in that totem pole, but it wasn't here. Go and bother those dreadful people at the museum."

Poole glanced at Brock with a mixture of concern and curiosity at how the inspector would react to his wife being called dreadful.

"I think we'll start with you, Mr Pentonville, and before you protest, we can either do this here or I can take you back to the station and throw you into a holding cell with someone who might well end up wearing your teeth on a necklace. It's up to you."

Simon Pentonville scraped his chair back across the oak floor as he rose and threw down his napkin. "This really is too much," he said as he passed Brock and Poole. "I've a good mind to talk to your chief inspector chap Tannock about this."

Brock laughed. "Good luck finding him, you'll have to go to every golf course in the county."

Simon headed out across the hall, and back into the study they had been in last night. Once they were all seated again, Brock began.

"I hear that you and your brother received a bit of a nasty shock in the will?" he said, clearly fishing.

Simon's eyes snapped to the inspector's. "What do you mean by that?"

Brock said nothing, but shrugged and smiled.

"You mean the debt?" Simon said, falling into the inspector's trap nicely. "We didn't know about it if that's what you mean. I knew this place was a bloody money pit, but I didn't think it mattered." He leaned back in his chair and looked up at the ceiling. "I always thought the old man had a load of cash hidden away somewhere. I had no idea we were basically broke."

"Do you know why your father left the totem pole to Ted Daley?"

"Not a clue, and I don't care. What would I do with a big lump of wood other than burning it?"

Poole frowned. There was something in his answer that was too quick, too rehearsed.

"Don't you think it's odd that your father only left that piece and none of the others in the barn?"

"Everything in there is junk, we're going to sell it all and hope it amounts to enough to give this place the lick of paint it needs before we can sell it."

"And this would be you and your brother, would it?"

Simon's eyes narrowed. "Clive and I are in agreement on this."

"Why didn't your father tell you the state the place was in financially?"

"My father didn't tell us much of anything," Simon said darkly. "We didn't see eye to eye."

"And why was that?"

"As my father became older, his head became firmly stuck in the clouds. He was always talking about what my grandfather had done—he was obsessed with it."

"And what had your grandfather done?"

"Wasted a load of bloody money, that's what." He looked at their blank expressions and sighed. "He travelled all over the world buying the junk that's in the barn and wasted most of the family's fortune doing it. By the time he died we were on our knees, then my father made some investments and got us back on our feet before he gave up on it all and started spending more and more time in that bloody barn."

"What was he doing in there?"

"I don't know!' Simon said, throwing his hands in the air. "Apparently he just wasted his time while the bank account went down, and here we are."

"And apart from your guests in the other room, were there any other visitors to the manor over the last week or so?"

"No, there weren't. Can I get back to my breakfast now?"

Brock stared at him as he pulled a boiled sweet from his pocket and popped it into his mouth.

"What is your relationship with Miss Kendall?"

"None of your bloody business," Simon said, standing up and marching around behind their chairs.

"Go on then, Mr Pentonville, you can go and finish your breakfast, but send in one of your friends when you do."

Simon grunted as he passed through the door and into the hall.

"This inheritance business is a strange one," Brock said the moment he had left. "I just can't get my head around him leaving that one piece to Ted Daley and it not meaning something. I need to check the value with Laura again, see if we're maybe missing something."

"He knows something about it he's not telling us," Poole added. "He couldn't have answered any quicker when you mentioned it."

"Glad you noticed." Brock grinned.

The door, which had slowly shut after Simon had left the room, swung open again to reveal Ellie Kendall.

"Now I hope you know that I didn't mean what I said in there, I was just being silly. Simon and Clive fight a bit, but what siblings don't, eh? Anyway, I'm sure I don't have anything of use to tell you, I've basically been holed up at the house apart from on Thursday."

"Why, what happened on Thursday?"

"Well, Simon arranged for us all to go out horse riding," Ellie answered, looking at them with her large, almost bug-like eyes.

"And was that on the estate?"

"Yes, we went out across the fields and then had a little race back."

"And how long have you known the Pentonvilles?"

"Oh, yonks. We've all been part of the black sheep bunch for ages."

"The black sheep bunch?" Poole asked, his pen pausing over the page of his notebook.

"Oh, it's just what we call ourselves," she said with a wave of her hand. "Our families all think we're brats and are tight with the money. That's why we're all here now; Simon and Charles are the first of us to be free!"

"You mean because their father died?"

She blinked and looked at them both. "Oh, obviously it's very sad," she said, barely bothering to attempt sincerity. "But he was old. Anyway, now we're all here until they can flog the place and hopefully pay for us all to go on some fab holiday or something!"

"So you're freeloaders?" Brock said bluntly.

She stared at him, a playful smile writhing on her lips. "Well, of course!" she said and shrugged before descending into another raucous laugh. "You don't expect someone like me to get a job, do you?"

Brock rolled the boiled sweet around his mouth and in the silence, Poole heard it clattering against his teeth.

"And are you and Simon an item?"

"An item!" Ellie roared. "Oh Inspector, you're so wonderfully old-fashioned! We're lovers, if that's what you mean, though I dare say it's a little more casual than whatever romantic notion you've got in your head." She gave another bray of laughter, her eyes sparkling.

"And how did Simon and his brother feel about their father dying, their inheritance?"

"Well like I said, they were finally bloody free, weren't they? If only my father would kick the bucket, then I wouldn't have to be such a dreadful scrounger."

She looked at Poole, saw the shocked expression on his face and smiled. "I'm sorry Sergeant, have I shocked you? I'm sure there must have been times when you wouldn't have minded your parents to pop their clogs?"

Poole said nothing but looked back to his notepad. His fingers gripped the pen so tightly that they turned white.

"Did I touch a nerve, Sergeant?"

"OK, that will be all. Can you send another of your friends through?" Brock said.

They remained in silence until she had left the room, then Brock turned to his partner. "Everything OK, Poole?"

"Yes, sir," Poole said, glad that his phone had begun to buzz in his pocket, giving him a reason to avoid further questioning.

He pulled it out and answered.

"We've found the hotel Clive Pentonville was booked into in London," Constable Roland Hale's voice said down the line.

"OK, so are you bringing him back here?"

"Not exactly, he never checked in."

Poole's eyes darted to Brock, who was studying him with a curious expression. "What do you mean never checked in?" Poole said as he watched Brock's eyebrows rise.

"The hotel he was booked into said he never turned up. If he went to London, he must have changed his mind and stayed somewhere else."

"OK, thanks, Roland." He hung up and turned to Brock.

"Let me guess, Clive Pentonville hasn't turned up in London?"

"No."

The door opened behind the inspector, and Helen Blaxon walked through. Her dark, darting eyes switched between the two of them, standing with her hands on her hips.

"I hope this won't take long, I really don't have much to tell you and I have a terrible headache."

"We only need to ask you a few questions at the moment, Miss Blaxon," Poole said, guessing that the inspector would have no chance of remembering her name.

"Well, good," she said haughtily, moving behind them and around the desk before sitting on the edge of the chair on the other side and leaning forwards. "Let's get it over with then."

"How do you know the Pentonvilles?" Brock asked.

"Jonathan knew Simon from the racing scene, we've been together about five years or so." She shrugged as though no further explanation was required.

"And what time did you arrive here?"

"Last Sunday," she answered flatly.

"And did you go anywhere near the barn during your stay here?"

"The barn? No. Why would I?"

"Were you aware of any difficulties Simon and Clive might have been having?"

"Difficulties? Not that I know of, no. I mean, everything's all rosy for them at the moment, isn't it? Inheriting all this?" She waved her hand around to convey Otworth Manor.

Poole waited for Brock to correct her, but instead, he simply nodded.

"OK, can you send Mr Finley in, please?"

She pursed her lips, got up and left the room.

Poole looked at Brock expectantly.

"These people don't want to talk to us," the inspector said slowly. "I think that they think we're beneath them, that we're just an inconvenience. The thing they don't seem to understand is, this is a murder inquiry, and I'll get what I bloody want from them. Clive Pentonville's got to be our number-one suspect now. Let's get the last one over with, and then we need to find him."

"Yes, sir," Poole replied as the door opened and Jonathan Finley stepped through.

He smiled at them and held his hands out, palm upwards. "How can I help you chaps?"

"Take a seat, Mr Finley," Brock said in a weary voice.

Jonathan moved around, took a seat behind the desk and leaned forward with his elbows on its surface.

"What time did you arrive at the manor?"

"Monday, with Helen," he said. "We just came for a few days to celebrate Simon's new freedom."

"You mean because of his father's death?"

"Yes." Jonathan smiled. "Do you think we're callous, Inspector?"

Brock stared at him for a moment, as though deciding something, and then spoke with a hard, flat tone. "Did you know that Simon and Clive aren't going to inherit much money?"

The smile froze slightly on Jonathan's face. "What do you mean?"

"I mean that William Pentonville left a pile of debt and a business that was barely breaking even."

Jonathan frowned. "But this place, surely?"

"The place is a money pit. They're not looking to sell because it will give them financial freedom, they're looking to sell so they can clear their father's debts."

Jonathan said nothing but stared at the desk in front of him with a kind of glazed expression on his face.

"Did you see anyone around the manor you hadn't seen before? Anyone who might have been acting suspiciously?"

"What?" he said, looking up. "No."

"I can imagine that the new information you've learned

here today might make you think about leaving, but I'm afraid I'm going to need you all to stay here for a few days until we can gather some more information on the case. Could you send Simon back in here a moment, please?"

"Right," Finley said, rising, still seemingly in a state of shock.

They watched him leave the room before Brock rose from his seat and stretched. "Right, here's the plan," he said as he cracked his knuckles. "Once we've filled Simon in on his missing brother, you're going to drop me off at Sal's. I'm then going to buy two of whatever is the biggest sandwich she makes and walk back to the station to take in a bit of sunshine after being cooped up in this mausoleum. You can go straight back to the station, get backgrounds on all this lot, and follow up on where the hell Clive Pentonville is."

"Yes, sir," Poole said, pondering again on how this case seemed to have unleashed the full force of Brock's appetite.

"What is it now?!" Simon said, bursting back through the door.

"Can you think of anywhere that your brother might have stayed in London? Friends, family?"

"I haven't got a bloody clue, we stay out of each other's way." He frowned at them both. "Why? Do you think Clive had something to do with this?"

"He booked himself into a hotel in London and never checked in."

"So you think he killed this chap and then scarpered?! Ha!" He threw his head back and laughed. "That is priceless!"

"And why exactly do you think this is so funny?" Brock asked quietly.

"Oh well, come on, Clive? I mean, if you knew him you'd know he'd never had it in him!"

"You'd be surprised what people are capable of in the right circumstances, Mr Pentonville. If your brother gets in contact with you, inform us immediately."

Brock stepped out into the hall and Poole followed.

The sun was climbing higher in the sky now, and the chill of the morning air had given way to a warm breeze and the buzzing of insects.

"When you get back to the station, put out an alert on Clive Pentonville as wanted in connection with a murder inquiry. If we can flush him out, we might start getting some answers on all of this."

CHAPTER TWELVE

"So, I hear you've got a body in a totem pole?" Anderson said with a sneer. "Is there anywhere you and Brock go where you don't turn up a dead body?"

"Afternoon, Anderson," Poole said as he poured himself a coffee from the battered old machine in Bexford Police Station canteen. "And what are you and Sharp working on at the moment? His golf swing? Or where he's going to have his next lunch with the captain on expenses?"

Anderson's wide jaw tensed, his chest pushed forward. "Keep talking like that, Poole. Things are going to change around here and then you might just regret talking like that."

"What do you mean?"

Anderson grinned. "Well, that's for you to find out, isn't it?" he said, before turning and walking away.

Poole finished making the two coffees and walked back to the office he and Brock shared in a thoughtful mood. Anderson with a smile on his face was never going to be a good sign, and he seemed to think there was some news afoot at the station. Something to worry about later.

"Ah! There you are," Brock said as he opened their office door. "Sorry, but when I got back and you weren't here, I decided to start." He took another bite of the huge sandwich, which was already half gone.

"What is it today?"

"Thinly sliced steak, three types of cheese, some sort of pickle that I swear has been made by the gods, honey-fried onions and a mustard mayonnaise."

"Bloody hell," Poole said, quickly placing the coffees down on each desk before jumping into his seat and unwrapping the wax paper torpedo that was sitting in front of him.

For the next few minutes, they were in silence, eating through their giant sandwiches without pausing for conversation. When they had finished, they sat and sipped at their coffees as Poole ran through the information he had had time to find while Brock had fetched lunch.

"So, the Pentonville history is pretty much what we've already heard from Laura. Grandfather sounds like he was a bit of a lad. Travelled the world, mostly attending parties of the rich and famous. William Pentonville was left with a big creaky old house and a load of debt. He turned it around and then set up the stables, which was sort of allowing the place to run itself."

"I thought Simon said they had debt?"

"Well they have, but I think he might have been over-egging it a bit. The stables have got a few debts, but that's because they added a few new stalls just before Christmas. They're full now though, so it should all pay for itself."

"Interesting. Maybe Simon Pentonville was just hoping for more of the good life than he's got. Go on."

"Ellie Kendall comes from old money," Poole continued. "The Kendalls have an estate up in the Lake District, the town up there is probably named after them, and she's an only child so she'll get the lot."

"From what she said," Brock interjected, "she's not getting it now."

"No, I'm guessing she's been cut off. Anyway, there's nothing in her background that leapt out. Helen Blaxon is a bit different."

"Oh yeah?"

"Well, she's not aristocracy, that's for sure. Her father was a headmaster and her mother was a nurse, but they were well off enough to send her to art college. Apparently, she made a bit of a stir there and came out as a bright new thing in the art world, only one problem." Poole looked up at the inspector, enjoying the expectant expression on his face.

'Well, come on!" Brock bellowed.

"She put on her first show and apparently it was a complete disaster. Bashed by the critics and left her a bit adrift in the art scene, apparently."

"Ouch, so her career has turned into a damp squib and now she's looking for a way to freeload as well."

'Maybe. Then there's Jonathan Finley. He comes from money, but not the old aristocracy like Ellie. His family runs a horse stable in Ireland. I spoke to someone who works there and Jonathan didn't have any interest in the family business, so they cut him off—his father wants him to make something of himself on his own."

"And how do they all know Simon?"

"Simon and Ellie went to university together at Oxford where they both flunked out, apparently. Simon met Jonathan through the racing scene like Helen said."

Brock nodded thoughtfully. "I think it's time we checked in with Sheila," he said, pulling his phone from his pocket and staring at it. "Oh, bloody hell! How do you do that speaker call thing again?"

"On that old thing?" Poole smiled. "Who knows, maybe put more coal in or something?"

Brock gave him a stare that could have melted glass as Poole pulled his own phone from his pocket and called Sheila.

"You're not going to like it," she said as soon as she answered, her voice projecting around the room from the small speaker on the back of the phone.

"I hate it when you say that," Brock said.

"No, you don't," Sheila said with a flat voice. "You love it, it makes it more interesting."

Brock grinned. "You've got me. OK, go on."

"There's basically nothing at the museum. Uniform didn't find any other points of entry that looked like they'd been broken into. So there wasn't much for us to look at there. We went over to the door to the alley, the one in the storeroom that someone tried to break in. Something a bit odd there."

"What?"

"Well, it looks like the lock actually gave way but then they didn't get in obviously. Maybe something scared them off, could have just been someone coming along the street."

"OK, and the barn?"

"Well, there are loads of prints in there. It's been used as a storeroom for decades, so it's not that surprising. Luckily we can roughly discount the older ones. We found fresh prints on the wall, right by where the totem pole was stored. Good thinking, checking there."

"Whose were they?"

"No one in the system, but I'll run them against the

suspects once we've gone around and taken all theirs. We're doing that today."

"OK, thanks, Sheila," Brock said.

Poole's finger moved to hang up when Sheila spoke again, this time hesitantly.

"Um, Sam."

"Yes?"

"You know I'll have to take Laura's fingerprints as well, right?"

Brock's face broke into a wide smile. "No problem," he said, laughing.

Poole hung up as he heard a sigh of relief from the other end.

"Well let's hope that fingerprint ends up being useful," Brock said, leaning back.

Poole watched him as he looked up at the ceiling, smiling.

Poole was fairly sure that on any normal day the idea of Laura being fingerprinted might well have riled Brock, yet today he had found it funny. He thought about the last couple of days and the inspector's wildly fluctuating mood. Combined with his sudden return to smoking and an overindulgence in food, something was up.

A thought rushed through Poole's mind, and he had opened his mouth and vocalised it before he could stop himself.

"Is Laura pregnant?"

Brock's grey eyes flicked towards him in surprise. "Bloody hell, Poole, not much gets past you, does it?! Yes, she is!" he cried out, as though he had been holding the news back with increasing difficulty all day. "It's very early days though," he added, trying to calm the manic smile on his face.

Poole grinned back at him. "Congratulations, sir," he said warmly. "I won't say anything to anyone else, don't worry."

Brock nodded and chuckled. "I just can't believe it. Me, a dad."

"You'll be great."

Brock looked up at him, the smile faltering. "You still haven't spoken to your mum, have you?"

Poole straightened up in his seat. "No, not yet."

"The longer you leave it, the worse it is. You can't let these things fester. Get it out in the open, find out what happened and move on."

"I'm not sure moving on is an option," Poole said darkly as he stared at the threadbare carpet.

"Well, it has to be," Brock answered. "You've already lost one parent; don't head straight into losing another one until you're sure."

Poole nodded but didn't look up.

"Come on then," Brock said, standing and moving towards the door. "Let's get back to it." There was a knock on the other side as he reached it and he opened it to find Constable Sanders.

"Sir, we've got an ID on our victim," she said, handing him a file.

Brock opened it and frowned as Sanita and Poole exchanged grins.

"Matt Pike," Brock said. "Someone in the Met spotted him, did they?"

"Yes, sir. He's got no record, but he's well known to them. Long been suspected of being a fence for stolen goods at the high end, big value stuff."

"And it says here that he runs an antique warehouse?" Brock said, looking at the file. "Well, that certainly makes things interesting," he said, looking up and smiling.

"You think he was here about the totem pole?" Poole asked.

"Maybe, but I'm starting to wonder if there's something else going on here. I think we should have another chat with Ted Daley back at the manor house. He's worked there the longest. If anyone knows the secrets of the place, he does."

CHAPTER THIRTEEN

Having first gone to the stables, Brock and Poole had been told by Lucy Flowers that Ted was "messing about in his sheds." She then directed them towards a small gathering of huts that were shielded from the manor house by a small copse of trees that was a good distance from the stables in the wide green expanse of the grounds.

"Nice little job this," Brock said as they skirted around the edge of the small clump of trees. "Out in the fresh air, working with the land."

"Yesterday you would have said it was a bloody nightmare. Working for some rich idiot who was born with a silver spoon in his mouth and didn't know anything about the real world."

Brock smiled. "Yesterday was a long time ago, Poole."

"Morning," Ted Daley said, looking up from the ride-on lawn mower he had been bent over as they approached. The front panel was open and the small engine inside revealed.

"Morning, Mr Daley," Brock said. "We've just got a few more questions for you."

"All right, all right," he replied, folding his arms and leaning back on the edge of the mower.

"When we spoke before you said that you didn't know what any of the stuff in the barn was worth?"

"That's right, I don't have a clue what's even in there, really."

"But has there ever been any hint that there might be something valuable on the property? Something William Pentonville might have hinted at?"

Ted frowned. "You're not talking about that Shakespeare rubbish, are you?"

Poole's pen hovered over his notepad. Next to him, Brock had tensed and when the inspector spoke again it was with urgency.

"What Shakespeare stuff?"

"It was old Edgar Pentonville who started it all, William's father. Got drunk in the pub one night down in the village and said he had something to do with Shakespeare that was worth a fortune. First book or something, I think they called it a folio. Anyway, caused all sorts of a stir it did, and the manor house was burgled twice afterwards. Rumour was he hid whatever it was, then."

"And did William ever talk about it?"

"No," Ted said slowly. "But now you mention it, when he said about the boys getting a surprise when he was gone, he did say something odd now I think of it."

"What?'

"He said that they wouldn't get their hands on the real prize. I thought he was talking about the manor, but then he gave them that, didn't he?"

"Yes, he did," Brock said thoughtfully. "OK, Mr Daley, I think that's all for now." Brock turned away and Poole followed.

"What are you thinking, sir?" he asked as they headed back around the trees. The sunlight filtered through and dappled the grass in front of them with shadow.

"I'm thinking there was something else in that totem pole."

"But they did an ultrasound on the thing, they would have seen if anything was in there, wouldn't they?"

"Not if it was thin and flat and stuck up against the wood —it would have just looked like part of the wooden back."

"Like a book?"

"That's what I'm thinking. William Pentonville knew his sons were both a bloody nightmare, but he left them the manor house."

"Which isn't in the best financial health," Poole added.

"No, he probably thought it would give them a chance to take on some responsibility. The big question is, what did he really leave Ted Daley? It's been bothering me that he would only leave him one thing. Why just that piece? What on earth was Ted Daley going to do with a bloody great totem pole? Especially if he is going to lose his home when the Pentonville brothers sell up or kick him out."

"So, he left him something else hidden in there? Like this Shakespeare book?"

"Could be," Brock said. "I don't know much about antiques, but if this thing was anything to do with Shakespeare, I'd guess it would be worth a fortune."

"And something worth killing over," Poole added thoughtfully.

"Yes. Let's go and see my lovely wife and see if she can give us an idea of what it might be."

CHAPTER FOURTEEN

"It depends," Laura Brock said, shrugging. She held a mug of green tea in her hands as she leaned on her kitchen table.

"On what?" Brock asked. He and Poole were also sitting at the table, tucking into a plate of chocolate biscuits and nursing tea of their own.

"On what it is, obviously. You can't just say 'Shakespeare book' and expect me to know what we're dealing with."

"Ted Daley said something about a first folio?" Poole added.

Laura looked at him sharply. "I think he's got that wrong," she said, shaking her head as though trying to free something from it.

"Why?"

"A Shakespeare first folio would be like finding the Holy Grail. It would be worth an absolute fortune, millions. Hold on." She got up and left the room, returning a few moments later with a laptop. She tapped away as the two men continued to make light work of the biscuits. "Here we go; *Mr William*

Shakespeare's Comedies, Histories, & Tragedies is the 1623 published collection of William Shakespeare's plays," she read aloud from the screen. Her finger worked the wheel of the mouse as she scrolled down the page. "It says here that one sold for 3.7 million in 2008." She looked up. "If they've found one of these, bloody hell." She leaned back and exhaled slowly.

"Sounds like something someone would kill over," Poole said.

"Well we won't know until we find it, but it could be long gone now," Brock said. "How would you go about selling something like that?"

Laura puffed out her cheeks. "It wouldn't be easy. That kind of thing is only going to be of interest to a few people, and I have no idea how you'd keep it a secret. This is big news."

"I'm guessing a dodgy antique dealer with a history of being involved with stolen goods might fit the bill," Poole said, turning to Brock.

"Matt Pike," Brock said, nodding.

"This is the man whom you found in the totem pole?" Laura asked.

"Yes," Poole answered. "Apparently he's got a bit of a reputation for handling high-end stolen items down in London."

"Oh," Laura said, sitting upright. "I almost forgot to tell you. Do you remember, Sam, we heard Jemima having a bit of an argument with Byron on the phone the night of the party?"

"Yes?"

'Apparently that was because Bryon wants to sell the totem pole already."

"Sell it?"

"I know, it makes no sense. Jemima said he was all enthusiastic about the museum getting it and then out of the blue, he says he wants to sell it."

"Let me guess," Brock said, smiling. "He'd had an offer too good to refuse."

"Yes, how did you know that?"

"I didn't, but I'm wondering if more people knew about this Shakespeare book than they're letting on."

"So you think someone tried to buy the totem pole thinking the folio might still be in there?"

"I think it's pretty likely. It also makes me wonder about the attempted break-in. Maybe someone tried to get at it before it left the manor house, and somehow Matt Pike got in the way and was killed for it."

"But why was Matt Pike even there? How did he know about it?" Poole asked. "Surely someone must have invited him there to try and sell the thing on?"

"Maybe, or maybe he got wind of it himself somehow?"

"Or he was supposed to be a partner and someone got greedy?" Laura said.

Brock smiled. "That's why I married her, Poole—sharp as a knife."

"I thought it was because of my stunning good looks?"

"That as well."

Poole looked down at his mug of tea, feeling slightly awkward.

"Oh Sam, you're making Guy feel awkward. Go on. Go and do some work."

"All right," Brock said, standing and looking at the yellow kitchen clock which hung on the wall. "I guess there's still time for us to go and find out who made Byron the offer for the pole. Have you got his address?"

Laura moved across to a drawer and pulled out an address book.

"Here you go," she said as she passed the book to Poole at an open page.

He noted it down, said goodbye, and moved out into the hall as Brock said goodbye to his wife.

"Who's this Byron then, sir?" he said as they stepped back out into the warm and still summer afternoon.

"Byron Lanister, he owns the museum, well, sort of. He inherited the building, but it's under a one-hundred-year license to the town to be used as a museum—his family tied the place up about fifty years ago."

"So he might be someone who wouldn't mind having a little windfall from selling the pole then?"

"I'd guess not, but according to Laura it wasn't worth very much, and he might think differently if he had known what had been in it."

"If the folio was in there, then whoever killed Matt Pike must have it."

"Maybe, but not necessarily. Someone could have killed Matt Pike afterwards and just used the pole to hide the body. Maybe they thought Matt Pike had double-crossed them and got there before them somehow. I'm starting to worry about Clive Pentonville not surfacing."

"It is starting to look like he's our man."

"Yes," Brock said slowly, "or another victim we haven't found yet."

They walked back up to the house in quiet reflection. Despite the warm afternoon, which rang with birdsong and seemed to glow with the golden light of the waning sun, there was a grim air surrounding the pair.

CHAPTER FIFTEEN

B yron Lanister's substantial house was situated on a street in a well-to-do part of Bexford. The large houses were all made from small, red bricks: a contrast to the yellow stone that made up most of the city. Each had a set of grey pillars forming a formal porch which had the effect of making the houses appear even grander than they were.

"Here we are, sir, number fourteen," Poole said, pulling the car over as it slipped out of gear for the third time on the short journey and gave a grinding screech.

"Bloody hell, Poole, can't we get a better car than this thing?" Brock grumbled as he heaved himself out with considerable effort.

"Doesn't sound like it, sir. I emailed the chief inspector like you said, but I didn't hear anything back."

A low rumble came from Brock as he leaned on the roof of the car and looked at Poole. "You wouldn't get a reply from an email, anyway. Tannock's as useless as me at all this tech stuff."

Poole ignored the fact that replying to an email was

hardly "tech stuff" and wondered instead at Brock's expression. "What is it, sir?"

"There are some changes coming at the station."

Poole's mind immediately jumped to his conversation with Anderson earlier that day.

"Anderson was gloating over something or other, what is it?"

Brock gave a small chuckle. "Well, I don't know what he's got to gloat about, it might not work out in the way he thinks it will."

"Sir?" Poole said, getting impatient.

"Tannock's retiring in a few months. Though I'm not sure what the difference will be really, he already spends more time on the golf course or having lunch than he does in the office."

"Retiring?" Poole said, leaning on the roof of the car on the opposite side to Brock and thinking about the ramifications of this. "Why would Anderson be happy about that?" he said, looking up.

"I'm guessing because he thinks that Sharp's going to get the job," the inspector answered. His grey eyes fixed on Poole as though conveying something to him.

"Have they asked you to take over, sir?" Poole said, speaking as though the inspector's eyes were handing him the words.

"They've asked me to apply," Brock said in a flat voice. "But I haven't made any decisions yet."

Poole nodded but said nothing.

"Right," Brock said, slapping the top of the car. "Let's go and see this Byron chap."

Poole locked the car manually as the remote lock had failed and started across the street after him. A movement to his right made him turn his head. A few hundred yards down the road a figure was standing, watching him. He paused and turned towards them. As soon as he did so, they turned and walked away.

"Come on, Poole!" Brock called from the garden path of the house.

Poole obeyed and ran across the road

He was halfway up the path when the door was opened by a middle-aged woman with red cheeks and grey hair, who was wiping her hands on a tea towel.

"Yes?" she asked suspiciously, as though she'd seen their kind before and weren't keen on them.

"I'm Detective Inspector Brock and this is Detective Sergeant Poole, we'd like to speak to Byron Lanister."

"Oh, right enough," she answered, her expression changing from one of suspicion to one of curiosity. "I'll go and get him, then. You can wait in the hall." The woman turned and headed off down the wide hall, returning a moment later with a man in his forties with brown hair that was flecked at the sides with grey.

"Mrs Tuppet tells me that you are from the police, and am I right in thinking you might be married to Laura Brock?" he said, looking at the inspector.

"I am," Brock answered.

"Lovely." Bryon gave a smile which then quickly turned to a frown. "I assume you are here to talk to me about the unfortunate man who was found in the museum the other day?"

"That's right," Brock answered, watching Mrs Tuppet hovering at the back of the hall and pretending to dust. "We really wanted to ask about an offer we believe you might have had for the totem pole you had recently acquired."

"Oh, yes, well I have to admit that was rather odd."

"Odd?"

"I mean we'd only just been given the piece by the man out at the manor, and almost the next day I had a phone call from someone offering to buy it."

"And you wanted to sell, by all accounts?"

Lanister's eyes darted between them. "Yes, well I realise it is not ideal for the museum, but you see the place has barely broken even over the last few years, no fault of your wife of course," he said quickly to Brock.

"Of course," Brock said in a slightly louder tone than Poole thought necessary.

"But it was a very good offer, money that could have kept the place going for a few years. I'm afraid that I'm rather tied up with the place due to the old family trust. I have to top up funds when it runs low, and although I'm fond of the old place, it is a burden."

"Who made the offer?"

Byron frowned. "I'm not sure I should reveal that I have a responsibility to maintain some privacy when..."

"This is a murder inquiry, Mr Lanister," Brock cut in. "I'm afraid if you withhold any evidence relating to it you will be charged with obstruction of justice or, worse, being an accomplice."

"Right," Lanister said, paling. "Well, in that case, it was Clive Pentonville."

"Clive Pentonville? You're sure?"

Byron nodded. "He said he couldn't bear to let the pole leave the family, and that he would compensate the museum handsomely for the inconvenience. I did try and negotiate a deal where the family could buy it back and it would still be stored at the museum, but he didn't seem willing to make such an arrangement."

"And when exactly did he make this offer?"

"It was on Thursday afternoon, around three I think."

"And have you heard from him since then?"

"No I haven't, I did try calling the number this morning but there was no answer."

"OK, thanks for your time," Brock said abruptly, before turning on his heels and leaving.

Poole gave Lanister a quick smile and a nod before following him down the drive.

"You tracked Clive Pentonville's phone from the number uniform got from Simon and it led nowhere, right?"

"Yes sir, last known location was near the manor house on Thursday. It hasn't reconnected since, so we guessed he'd turned it off for some reason."

"Then I think it's time we did a full sweep of the grounds with dogs. We'll arrange it for tomorrow morning."

"You think Clive is there somewhere?"

"If he is, I don't think he's going to be alive. If he's not, then there's a good chance he's our killer."

CHAPTER SIXTEEN

"Is this really necessary?"

"Ah, Mr Pentonville, I'm glad you've decided to join us," Brock said, smiling at Simon who was standing at the top of the steps to the manor house with his hands on his hips. "Have you by any chance heard from your brother, yet?"

Simon Pentonville frowned and then sauntered down the steps towards them.

"Is that why you're doing this? Searching the grounds?" He swallowed and took a step backwards, his eyes gazing out across the land which swept away from them. The annoyance he had shown upon emerging had been replaced by anxiousness.

"Do you think something's happened to my brother?"

"A man has been murdered on your property, Mr Pentonville, and your brother is missing. I'm hoping those two things aren't related, but the longer he is out of contact, the more unlikely that scenario seems."

Poole watched the effect this had on Simon Pentonville closely. There was a jolt of something that resembled emotion there, but it was restrained and controlled almost immediately.

Pentonville cleared his throat and turned away from them towards the house. As he reached the top of the steps, a shout from across the lawn made him pause and turn around.

Poole turned too and saw a constable running across the short grass. He stepped out from the paving slabs onto the cool grass to meet him. "What is it, Constable?"

"We've found something, sir!"

"Where?"

"Over in the trees around the back of the manor, by the gardening sheds."

"What is it?" Simon Pentonville shouted from the top of the steps, his face pale.

"Please stay back in the house, Mr Pentonville," Brock shouted over his shoulder as he advanced towards Poole and the constable. "We'll inform you of anything we find as soon as we can."

Brock told the constable to lead the way and headed off after him. Poole hesitated for a moment and watched Simon Pentonville, who looked as though he was going to follow them, but then turned and stormed back into the house.

CHAPTER SEVENTEEN

"That looks like Clive Pentonville all right," Poole said as he and Brock stared down at the body that lay in the grass, half covered with twigs and leaves.

He looked up towards the edge of the treeline where the gardening sheds could be seen between the trunks. "We must have walked right by him when we talked to Ted Daley."

"We can't check every place we go for bodies, Poole," Brock said. "Anyway, the way he was covered with sticks and leaves, you'd have had to have been right on top of him to see." He sighed and put his large hands behind his head. "The problem we've got now is our prime suspect has turned out to be a victim."

"Do you think they were killed at the same time, sir?"

"It looks like he's been whacked over the head so maybe, but we'll wait for Ron to have a look before we can think about that. One thing I'll say, though; this is a fair distance from the barn." He turned and looked back through the trees towards the large house in the distance. "I think we'd better go and talk to the guests at the house again." He gave a brief instruction to a constable to let him know when the coroner and crime scene arrived and turned away towards the house. "We need a bloody golf cart to get us around this place," he muttered, before hitching his trousers up and getting back to business. "Tomorrow I want you to get the constables back onto everyone who works at the stables and keeps their horses there, double-check if anyone saw anything at all. I know they came up with nothing last time, but you never know. And we need to speak to Ted Daley and Lucy Flowers again as well."

"Yes, sir." Poole stared off into the distance, deep in thought.

"What is it, Poole?"

"Clive Pentonville, sir. He tried to buy the totem pole on Thursday afternoon, so he was alive then."

"Yes."

"Which means he didn't have the Shakespeare folio then."

"I'd guess not."

"But it means he knew where it was by then, surely?"

"Well, yes."

"So how does Matt Pike fit into this? If Clive Pentonville knew the Shakespeare folio was in the totem pole, he could have just come down here, opened the thing up and taken it. If he was careful, no one would have been the wiser. But he can't have tried to do that or he would have found Matt Pike's body in there."

"Unless he looked before Matt Pike was killed." Brock shrugged. "Or maybe he found the body or stumbled across the killer, who silenced him." He said this with a questioning tone and glanced at Poole as they walked.

"No, that wouldn't work," Poole said, shaking his head. "If Clive Pentonville rang Bryon Lanister to try and buy the pole, he must have already looked to know it was in there. And he can't have called if he was dead."

"Quite right, Poole," Brock said, smiling.

Poole looked at him and realised he was being tested again. He smiled slightly to himself, glad he seemed to have passed the test.

The manor house door was open when they arrived, and they stepped into the hall without waiting to be invited. They could hear voices coming from the dining room to the left, and so moved towards it until Brock stopped them both with a raise of his hand. They waited for a moment, listening.

"I just don't see what the point of dragging my brother into this is." Simon Pentonville's voice echoed down the hallway. "Helen can tell them about this old man she saw if she wants to, but Ellie, I think you should just stay quiet."

"I agree." Jonathan Finley's voice joined in. "We all need to stick together, and although he's a prize prat, Clive is one of us."

There was a murmuring of agreement, and Brock gave the signal for them to continue. He burst into the room, pushing the heavy door back with one thick arm so that it slammed back against the wood-panelled wall.

"Mr Pentonville," he boomed, standing next to the dining chair nearest the door where Simon was positioned. Simon turned to him, his face set in a grim, grey fashion.

"What is it?"

"I'm afraid we've found a body on the property," Brock said. Ellie Kendall gave a small yelp and clasped her hand over her mouth.

Simon rose to his feet and stared at Brock, his eyes burning. "And is it Clive?"

"We don't know, but if you are available tomorrow, we'd

like you to come along to the station to help us with identification."

Simon nodded and slumped back into his chair. "You think it's him, don't you?"

Ellie rose from her seat and moved behind him, resting her hands on his shoulders.

"It's too early to say," Brock said again. "Miss Kendall, perhaps I could talk to you in private?"

"Me?" Ellie said, her hand moving to her chest in surprise.

The four of them exchanged looks and Jonathan Finley rose unsteadily from his chair. "Now look here, Brock, a man has just lost his brother and we've all had a bit of a shock, so I think you can wait to ask your silly little questions until later."

Poole watched the man sway slightly, a large glass of brandy in his hand. The suave, good-looking appearance he had had when they had last seen him seemed to have been replaced by one of drunken dishevelment.

"I'm afraid, Mr Finley, that this can't wait. I have reason to believe that all of you are conspiring to withhold evidence in a murder inquiry."

There was another small yelp from Ellie Kendall, who then said, "Oh my goodness!"

"Be quiet, Ellie," he replied over his shoulder. He stared back at Brock. "You were bloody listening at the door, weren't you?! Like a peeping Tom!"

"As I seem to have to keep reminding you all, this is a murder inquiry. Everything is my business, and I will do whatever it takes to find whoever killed Matt Pike and the second victim."

"Matt Pike?" Simon said, his head turning towards them rapidly.

"You know him?" Poole asked.

"Um, he went to school with my brother," Simon said, his voice distant and confused. "You mean he was the chap in the totem pole?"

"We believe so," Brock answered, his large brow furrowed in thought. "Can you think of any reason he might have been here?"

"No," he answered quickly. "I mean, he must have been visiting my brother, but I wouldn't know why."

"Maybe he had a reason to contact him again?" Brock said.

Poole's eyes scanned the four people facing them, looking for any sign of recognition in what Brock had said, but there was nothing.

"What do you mean?" Simon said blankly.

"Miss Kendall, if we could speak to you first?" Brock said, turning to her.

"Oh, lord!" Ellie said, grinning and moving from behind Simon.

"I'm coming with you, you've no right to question her on her own," Simon said, standing up with her.

For a brief moment, Poole thought Brock was going to arrest Pentonville just for getting in the way, but then his expression changed.

"As you all seem to have been discussing the case between you in any case, maybe we will do this all together. Sit down, both of you."

They both took their seats again on autopilot at the tone of the inspector's command.

"Miss Kendall," Brock said, turning to Ellie, now seated again at the other side of the table. "I believe you have some information relating to Clive Pentonville which you have not yet shared with us?"

Ellie looked at the other three in turn, settling on Jonathan.

"It doesn't matter to Clive now, does it?" Finley said in an aggressive tone, taking another large swig of brandy. "He's bloody worm food by the sounds of it."

"Shut it, Finley," Simon snarled.

Ellie's wide eyes darted around the room before locking onto the inspector's. "I saw Clive on Thursday after we'd gone off riding. That was the day that man was killed, wasn't it?" she asked, her head tilting slightly on one side like a bird.

"It was, yes," Brock said, turning to Simon. "I thought you said your brother had gone to London?"

"I thought he had," he answered sullenly.

"Maybe you're mistaken?" Brock asked, turning back to Ellie.

"No," she answered firmly. "It was definitely him."

"Where did you see him?"

"When we went for our ride. We were heading out towards the back end of the estate when I realised I'd left my phone back at the house. The others waited while I headed back to get it and I saw Clive when I was riding back to them."

"Where was he? What was he doing?"

"He was walking down towards the stables from the house."

"And why were you so reluctant for us to hear this, Mr Pentonville?" Brock said, turning to him.

"Why the bloody hell do you think? Clive told us all that he was in London, then there's this bloody murder and then Ellie said she'd seen him here all along! What did you expect us to think?"

"You thought your brother had killed Matt Pike?"

"Of course not!" Simon said, his hand slamming onto the tabletop in front of him as he spoke. "I didn't even know it was Matt Pike in there, did I? And I know Clive wouldn't have been involved in anything like that, anyway! All I knew was that someone had been killed down in the barn, and I didn't think it would look good for Clive if you knew he'd been there. Anyway, it's this old man that Helen saw that you should be looking into."

"And what old man would this be, Miss Blaxon?" Brock asked, turning to her. She looked up at him, her eyes blinking furiously.

"We were having an argument about which path back was quicker, and so Simon suggested we all take a different one and then we'd see. So we all went off on our own. I was coming back around along the river at the bottom of the estate and was going to come up past the stables, but my horse got something stuck in his foot and I had to walk him back."

"And you saw someone as you made your way back?" Poole asked.

"I did, yes. There was a man in a navy-blue duffel coat, he had bright white hair, glasses and a white beard. I can't tell you much more than that though."

"And where exactly was this?"

"It was near the lodge on the south side, between there and the stables."

"And what was he doing?"

"Just walking as far as I could tell. He was a fair way away from me, but he nodded at me as though to say hello."

"And presumably you arrived back to the manor after the others?"

"Yes, I did. I headed straight for the stables as the horse was hurt and then walked up to the manor."

"And did you see anyone else around the stables at that time?"

"No."

"And do you know of anyone who might have been on the estate who would fit that description?" Brock said to Simon Pentonville.

"No, closest to it would be old Ted, but Thursdays are his day off, and Lucy's for that matter. Anyway, it's pretty clear that whoever it is must have killed this Matt Pike, and—" He trailed off, his eyes glassy.

"Clive must have arranged to meet Matt without telling me for some reason," Simon continued, his voice strained. "Then, maybe he stumbled onto the killer."

Brock looked around the room. The four of them were sitting in silence, each of them taking sips from their drinks occasionally.

"And which of you had heard of the Shakespeare folio that Simon's grandfather had reportedly hidden somewhere on the property?"

"Oh for goodness' sake!" Jonathan said, throwing back his head. "What on earth has that got to do with anything?! It's just a stupid bloody story."

"And yet it seems as though Clive Pentonville contacted an old friend of his, Matt Pike, who just happened to specialise in antiquities."

Jonathan's mouth opened and then closed again. "You mean Clive thought this Shakespeare thing was real? And he was trying to sell it off under Simon's nose without him knowing?! Well, that's a damn cheek I can tell you."

"Mind you," Ellie giggled, apparently back to her old self. "Simon's going to get the lot now, so I don't suppose it matters very much!" She stifled another braying laugh, and Jonathan gave a low chuckle with her.

Poole watched Simon, who was staring at the floor.

"I think that will do for tonight," Brock said, clapping his hands together. "I'll send someone around tomorrow to get a formal statement from you, Miss Blaxon, and there will be people here working and protecting the scene until late. I still want all of you to stay here for the time being."

"Wouldn't dream of being anywhere else." Jonathan waved his glass.

"I'll send a car around to pick you up for the identification, Mr Pentonville."

"Don't bother, I'll drive."

"If you like. The earlier the better, please."

Simon said nothing but continued to stare at the dark wood of the floor in front of him.

"I'm sorry, I realise how difficult this must be," Brock said, before turning towards the door with Poole in tow.

"I'm going to call it a night, Poole," Brock said when they were back out into the dusk of the evening. "I want to spend some time with Laura. I'd like you to make sure things here get done. Ron and Sheila need to inspect the scene and body, and I want uniform stationed there all night to make sure no one wanders across it. Tomorrow morning I want the whole area between that copse and the barn searched. If they did move the body there, something might have been dropped on the way that will give us a clue."

"Yes sir," Poole said. "Do you want me to drop you back first?"

"Don't worry, I'll get a lift from uniform. One more thing, though; I think we should look at the exact wording of this will that William Pentonville left. Find out exactly how the totem pole was left to Ted Daley. We'll talk to the lawyer tomorrow."

After watching the inspector leave a few minutes later in

a patrol car, Poole began walking back towards the small copse of trees, enjoying the cool air on his face.

No matter how horrific the circumstances, he was glad of work to set his mind to. His mother would be arriving home tomorrow, and anything that could distract him from the enormity of facing up to what he now knew about her was welcome.

CHAPTER EIGHTEEN

Poole woke to the sound of his phone alarm blasting a dull tone and vibrating on his bedside table. He leaned over and switched it off before rubbing the sleep from his eyes.

Despite being exhausted when he had finally arrived home the night before, he hadn't slept well. The impending confrontation with his mother passed through his mind every time he felt the soft embrace of sleep.

Almost as the thought came to him, he heard the front door of his flat open. A heavy weight seemed to drop in his stomach. She was home.

He climbed out of bed and threw some clothes on before stepping out into the main room of the flat.

"Hi, love."

"Hi," he said, watching her bustle about in the kitchen where she was placing various pots and jars in the fridge from two large hessian bags.

"I picked up a few bits from the shop they had there. It's all organic and locally made."

"Great," Poole said, his voice feeling tight in his throat.

She turned to him, pausing with a jar of chunky peanut butter halfway to the fridge. She sighed, put the jar in and closed the door.

"I know I've outstayed my welcome, Guy, you've been very kind letting me stay this long, I know it's been a pain. Anyway, you don't have to worry any more. Do you remember my friend Angela? Well, she's finally left her Derek, lazy slob that he is. She's looking for a fresh start and so we thought we might get a place here together."

"Oh, right," Guy said, slightly thrown by the sudden news. It was true that he had been desperate for his mum to move out even before he had discovered her role in the incident that had changed her life, but it was the last thing on his mind right now.

"Look," he said, his voice wavering. "We need to talk about something."

"OK," Jenny Poole said, her face a mixture of confusion and apprehension.

"Did you go and talk to the drug gang that Dad was working for?"

The colour drained from her face, and she reached out and grasped the kitchen countertop to steady herself.

"I—" She closed her eyes and her head bowed, shaking as it did so.

"I need to know what happened," Poole said, blood pounding in his ears.

"I just... I just wanted it all to stop!" she said, her voice breaking as her eyes filled with tears. "Your father didn't know what he was getting into at first and by the time he realised, they wouldn't let him go."

"You told me it was all his fault," Poole said coldly. He could feel the lead weight of worry turning to a fiery rage.

"It was his fault! He put us all in danger! He's the one who got mixed up in it all, he's the one who let it all go on too long."

"But you're the one who went and spoke to them and told them to let him get out of it."

"Yes! I was trying to help! I just wanted us all to be away from it so we could not be bloody terrified of opening the door every day!"

"But what happened to us, Simon dying, me getting shot. That was your fault."

He watched the puzzlement in her eyes. She shook her head. "No, I was just trying to help! That wouldn't have made them do that. Jack said it was something he'd done, he'd tried to leave them and had left them in a tight spot."

A shock like a bolt of lightning shot through him. His mother had no idea what she had done. She had no clue that when she had approached the gang members to release her husband from his commitments, she had approached the wrong gang. He and his friends had been shot at because another drug gang was bad for business, in retaliation, but she had never known it happened because of her.

He decided at that moment, he didn't want her to know.

He never wanted her to know.

"He did," Poole said. "He admitted it to me."

She took a step towards him and then stopped.

They paused in silence, neither of them knowing what to say next.

"I need to get to work," Poole said, turning back towards the bathroom.

"You need to stay away from your father, Guy. He'll only drag you down with him."

Poole said nothing.

CHAPTER NINETEEN

"For goodness' sake, can you just stop fussing, Sam!" Laura flicked him away with her hand as he tried to lift the pan of porridge from the stove for her.

"I'm just trying to help," Brock answered defensively.

"Maybe you should have thought of that during the last twelve years we've been together?" she said, laughing.

"Ouch," Brock said, feigning hurt feelings, his hand over his heart.

"So why won't you talk to me about this promotion?" she asked when he was sitting back at the kitchen table and stroking Indy's ears. The dog pushed his head into Brock's hand, his eyes closed.

"Not much to talk about. They've asked me to apply, I'm thinking about it."

"You know, most people would be over the moon if they were offered a promotion like that."

"Yes, but most people are idiots," Brock answered gruffly.

Laura turned to him and raised an eyebrow.

"Sorry," he muttered back.

When he had arrived back from the manor house yesterday evening, with the initial glow of being a soon-to-be father wearing off, he had moaned.

Moaned about the group of idle rich who were currently in residence there, moaned about the constable who had driven him home and how poor his driving had been, and had even moaned that Indy had taken his slipper off to his bed and drooled on it.

Laura had then, in no uncertain terms, told him that he needed to cut out this doom and gloom or they were going to end up with a child as grumpy as he was.

Sam Brock had taken this news to heart and was now determined to become an altogether sunnier figure. He realised he had slipped already.

"I don't just want to sit behind a desk," he said, sighing. "Meetings, red tape, looking over reports of other people doing real police work. It's just not me."

"Well then, it sounds like you've made your mind up to me," Laura said, turning and placing two bowls of porridge on the table.

"But things are different now," Brock said quietly, poking at the bowl in front of him with a spoon.

"You mean because of the lime?"

Brock looked up in confusion. "The lime?"

"I've got this new app on my phone which tells you the baby's size each week. Right now it's the size of a lime."

Brock got up, walked over to the fridge, and pulled a lime from the shelf in the door.

"Bloody hell," he said, holding it up.

"Anyway, why would that make you want to take the job? I know we're not rolling in it, but we're OK for money, aren't we?"

"It's not that," Brock said, putting the lime back and returning to his seat.

Laura stared at him as he finally took a spoonful of porridge. "The cursed detective," she said quietly. The spoon paused en route to his mouth, but he didn't look up. "That's it, isn't it?" she continued. "You're worried about being involved in cases. You think you should take the job because you'll be safer."

Brock looked up at her and gave a weak smile. "You can see right through me, can't you? A man afraid to do his job."

Laura looked at him for a moment, frowning in thought before leaning her spoon against her bowl. "You know what?" She folded her arms. "Bravery isn't about not being scared of anything. Bravery is about being afraid but doing it, anyway. You couldn't stop doing what you do to go and push paper around. You love what you do, no matter how much you moan about it."

Brock laughed and shook his head. "You are quite something, you know."

"I know." Laura smiled back, picking up her spoon again.

Brock got up, moved around the table and kissed her. "Your porridge could use some work, though," he said to her. "It's going to need golden syrup." He fetched some from the cupboard as Laura called him something rude.

"You know why you're thinking about it more?" she said when he was back at the table.

"Why?"

"Because of Guy."

"Well, yeah, I've lost two partners already, I don't want to lose a third."

"It's not just that," she said, smiling. "You like him. You've got this father-son thing going on."

"Bloody hell Laura, I'm not that old!"

"Oh, you know what I mean. I think you'd miss him if you took the promotion."

"Yeah well, Poole's all right." He shrugged.

Laura watched him and smiled.

CHAPTER TWENTY

"You've spoken to your mother," Brock said as soon as Poole appeared at the entrance to Bexford Station. He had called his young partner from the car park and told him to meet him there.

"Yes," Poole answered as he jogged down the steps to where the inspector was standing.

"Well?" Brock asked.

"I don't think she knows what she did. I don't think she knows she went to the wrong people and got us all in trouble."

"And you didn't tell her?"

"No," Poole said. He shook his head and turned away, conscious of his eyes, which were still red from tears shed on the short drive over. "I couldn't do it to her. I couldn't have her living with what that would mean. Me getting shot, Simon dying."

"You did the right thing."

"Maybe." Poole shrugged, wiping his eyes quickly with his sleeve. "But what does this mean for my dad? He's still to blame for getting us all involved in the first place, but he's only as responsible as Mum is for what actually happened to us."

"Talk to him, then," Brock said in a matter-of-fact voice. "See how you feel. In any case, he might be someone worth asking about Matt Pike."

Poole couldn't help but laugh. "Because all criminals know each other?!"

"No," Brock said, smiling. "Because all criminals know someone who knows someone else who knows everyone. Come on, let's go and see what bloody Ron Smith has to say for himself."

"I've been thinking, sir," Poole said as they headed across the car park towards the pathologist's office.

"Don't strain yourself, Poole."

Poole grinned at the slight. Whenever Brock was worried or concerned about somebody else, he invariably showed it by mocking them.

He could already feel the stress and sadness of the situation with his family fading into the background as the case and Brock's easy company took to the fore.

"The guests at the manor all had this race to see who could get back first when they were on their horse ride," Poole continued. "If they all went different ways, doesn't that mean that none of them can vouch for any of the others until they got back? I looked at the map of the estate on my phone and checked where they said they started. The four paths wind off in different directions and there's no clear line of sight between any of them, too many hills and trees. They're all roughly the same length, but it's quite a way back to the manor house."

"If anything, that gives them all an alibi," Brock said, as

they arrived at the entrance to the council building where Ronald Smith's office was located.

"Ah," Poole said, his finger rising in the air. "But the paths wind and bend all over the place. Someone could have left it and headed straight down along the little stream that runs almost all the way back towards the manor and made it back well before the others."

They walked along the corridor in silence for a while.

"If one of them did do it, it would mean they must have known about the Shakespeare folio in the totem pole," Brock said doubtfully.

"Yes, but they might have worked it out. You have been saying how strange you found it that William Pentonville left Ted Daley the pole in his will. Remember what William had said to Ted? That his two sons were going to have a shock coming to them?"

Brock stopped as they reached the door to Ronald Smith's office.

"You mean that William Pentonville knew that the estate was a money pit, but deliberately gave the only thing of real value to Ted Daley and not his sons. The Shakespeare folio that was hidden in the pole?"

"It's a thought, isn't it?"

"It is indeed, Poole. It is indeed."

Brock rapped on the door and opened at the same time as Ronald's voice rang out to come in.

"What have you got for us, Ron?" the inspector said, slumping into the left-hand chair of the two that faced the desk.

"And hello to you too, Sam." His beady eyes glistened with joy at having a captive audience. "Keeping well, are you?"

"Marvellous," Brock replied flatly.

"And you, Poole? All settled in here, are you?"

"Yes," Poole said, his voice flat, "so, what can you tell us about this victim?"

Ronald's smile froze slightly on his face as Poole cut the small talk off at the knees. "It looks as though he was killed with the same weapon," he said primly, adjusting some papers in front of him. "And if that crowbar you found by the barn hadn't been clean, I'd have been pretty sure it would have been that."

Poole noted this down and waited for Brock's next question. When it didn't come, and Ronald stayed silent, he turned to the inspector.

Brock's eyes sparkled, unseeing. "And how long do you think he had been there?" he said slowly.

Ronald stared back at Brock, a slight smile playing at the corner of his mouth. He had clearly noticed the reaction as well.

"Is there something bothering you, Sam? Something you've thought of, maybe?"

Brock got up suddenly, making Ronald jump back in his seat in fright.

"Just tell me how long you think he was there and then send the report over to me. I need to go."

"I'd say around the time that our first victim, Matt Pike, died. Thursday afternoon."

Brock grunted and turned out of the door. Poole jumped up and headed after him, leaving Ronald Smith looking puzzled.

"What is it, sir?" Poole gasped as he ran to keep up with Brock, who was striding down the corridor at pace.

"I'm wondering if we've been looking at this all wrong," he answered without slowing.

"How do you mean, sir?"

The inspector burst through the door and back out into the car park. "Where are you parked?"

"Over there," Poole answered, and then followed Brock as he headed off in the direction he had pointed.

"It's just occurred to me that the crowbar we found by the barn isn't the only one we've seen while we've been working on this case."

Poole frowned and his pace slowed as he thought about what the inspector could mean. He ran through the places that seemed likely in his head. The stables, the gardening sheds where Ted Daley seemed to spend most of his time. He couldn't remember seeing a crowbar in any of them.

It came to him as he reached the parked Ford Mondeo that Brock was already leaning on, waiting for him.

"You mean the one at the museum? The one we used to open the totem pole?"

"Exactly," the inspector answered as they climbed in and Poole fired up the stuttering engine.

"But how could that have been the murder weapon? Unless..." He glanced at the inspector as he pulled the car out of the space. "You mean Matt Pike might have been murdered at the museum after all?"

Brock was staring through the windscreen as though he was looking at some far-off TV screen. "What was the description Helen Blaxon gave of the man she had seen on the grounds of the manor?"

Poole pulled out into the slow-moving traffic of rush hour in Bexford before he answered. "She said he was an older gentleman, white hair and a white beard, I think. Why?"

"Down here," Brock said, pointing as they came to a junction. "We're going to the museum. There's someone there who fits that description, and I'd like to know if it was him down at the manor on the day Matt Pike was killed and if it was, why."

"Frazer Mullins!" Poole said, his voice rising in surprise. "Surely not. What reason would he have to kill Pike?"

"Who knows," Brock answered, his voice low. "But I want to get another look at that crowbar."

"We used it to open the totem pole, we'd have noticed if it had any blood on it."

"It could have been cleaned."

Poole nodded, his mind now racing with these new possibilities.

CHAPTER TWENTY-ONE

"What do you want to see Frazer for?" Nancy Cole said. The museum receptionist was wearing her usual black clothing, but a streak of red had appeared in her hair since they had last seen her.

"Police business," Poole said, deciding that he should be the one to push this. The inspector's wife worked here. These people were her colleagues.

"Well, he's not in today." Nancy shrugged.

"I thought he was always in?" Brock grumbled.

"First time he's ever called in sick apparently, that's what Jemima said this morning, anyway."

"OK, well we're going to need to go and look in your storeroom," Poole said.

"I'm going to have to ask Jemima about that," Nancy answered, looking doubtful.

"Then hurry it up!" Brock snapped. Nancy jumped out of her seat and headed off through a door behind her, giving the inspector a hard stare as she did so.

"Sir," Poole said quietly. "We might want to show a little bit of discretion here, you know, for Laura."

"Oh, don't worry about me, Guy," Laura's voice came from over his shoulder. "I'm made of sterner stuff." She stopped on the other side of the reception counter and folded her arms, glaring at her husband. "What exactly is going on?" she said as Nancy arrived behind her.

"We need to go down into the storerooms again, just briefly," Brock said flatly, holding her gaze.

"Why?"

"We think there may be something there that can help us with our enquiries."

Poole noticed Laura's expression harden at this standard police officer's response.

"Nancy said you wanted to see Frazer?" she said coldly.

"He phoned in sick today, I hear?" Brock said.

Poole noticed something pass across Laura's face; worry, maybe?

"It is unlike him. Do you think I should go around and see if he's OK?" she asked.

"No!" Brock said, his voice suddenly loud and making them all jump.

Laura's eyes widened. "You think he's a suspect, don't you?!"

"We'd just like to speak to him, Laura. There are some things we need to ask."

"Like what?"

The inspector sighed and stepped forward, putting his hands on her shoulders. "Laura, we need to see in that storeroom."

She nodded and embraced him for a moment before pulling away. "Jemima's gone out, but I've got the key. Come on."

She moved around the desk and headed towards the main room of the museum where Brock and Poole followed her in silence.

There were several visitors milling around as they passed through the large main room with its ornate, echoing roof. A young couple with large backpacks on were staring at a display that showed a map of Roman settlements in the area, and a small group of schoolchildren were gathered around a large dinosaur bone that had been found in the county.

They left the bustle of the room and headed through the small door that led into the storeroom. As soon as they stepped through, Brock and Poole looked to their right and saw a crowbar. It was in the same place they had found it when they had borrowed it to open the totem pole just a few days ago.

Poole moved to it and bent down to inspect it.

"What are you looking for?" Laura asked, her voice hesitant, as though she was unsure that she wanted to know the answer.

"Blood," Brock replied bluntly.

"But that's the crowbar we used to open the pole, isn't it?" Laura said, peering at it. "I think we would have noticed if it had been used to smash someone over the head with."

Poole pulled a plastic evidence bag from his pocket. It was far too small to house the crowbar, but he folded it back over his hand like a glove and picked the thing up. "I can't see anything, sir."

"OK, let's get it to Sheila first," Brock said. "She'll be able to use that blue light to see if there's any blood trace on it. Then we can send it to the lab to see if they can get any DNA from it." The inspector turned to his wife. "It might be nothing, but we need to check it."

She nodded, but still seemed confused by the whole situation.

"Have you had the alarm company out about the break-in?" he continued.

"We did, yes," she answered. There was a hesitancy in her voice that made Brock's eyebrow rise. "They said they couldn't find anything wrong with the system."

"Nothing wrong?" Brock said, looking at her.

Laura exhaled slowly and looked down at the floor. "They said that the doors at the back of the room that were forced should have triggered the alarm anyway, even if no one got in. They are looking into it. The chap from the security company said he thought it was probably just some malfunction they couldn't pick up yet. He said he'd come back and do some more thorough tests."

"And was Frazer there to hear this?"

"He was, yeah, it was yesterday afternoon." She caught the look in her husband's eye. "I just didn't think to tell you as I couldn't see what it had to do with the man in the pole! You told me you thought he'd been killed back at the manor house!"

"It's all right," Brock said, brushing a stray lock of her shoulder-length hair from her face. She smiled and took his hand in hers.

"Was Frazer here at the museum on Thursday?"

"Yes, definitely," Laura said before suddenly recoiling back. "Oh! Well, he did have a long lunch that day. He said he had errands to run. He was gone for a few hours."

"Right," Brock said, nodding slowly.

"Bloody hell, Sam, you don't really think he did this, do you?"

Brock sighed. "We'd better go," he said, leaning forward and kissing Laura on the forehead. "I'll see you at home."

CHAPTER TWENTY-TWO

Frazer Mullins lived in a block of flats situated at the edge of a small commercial estate at the edge of town. They had dropped the crowbar off at the station and a slightly irritable Sheila was making her way in on a Sunday to look at it, after having spent a long night out at the manor. Rather than wait for the results, they had driven out to the address Laura had given them for the museum worker.

"I don't know why," Poole said as they climbed from the car, "but for some reason, I pictured Frazer Mullins living in a small cottage somewhere. You know, in the country."

"He does like to give off that kind of impression, doesn't he?" Brock leaned on the edge of the car and looked up at the flats. "Like he's a wise custodian of the museum."

Poole looked at him. "You don't like him, do you?"

"It doesn't matter whether I like him or not," Brock grunted as he moved from the car. "He's a suspect. Let's just see what he's got to say for himself."

They headed across the small car park that was littered with weeds growing through the splits and cracks in the concrete. The day was heating up. The early morning haze that had drifted about as Poole had first arrived at the station had given way to a blue sky and an increasingly powerful sun.

They were glad of the cool shade provided by an overhanging porch at the front of the building as Poole scanned the list of names on the intercom next to it. He pressed the button next to Mullins and a small buzz rang out.

"Hello?" came the suspicious Scottish tones of the museum's caretaker.

"Frazer? It's Sam Brock here," he paused for a moment before continuing, "in an official capacity. We need to have a quick word with you."

The pause this time was from the other end of the line.

"I'm not feeling too well," Frazer said weakly. "Can you come back another time?"

"I'm afraid we can't, no."

There was another pause before the buzz and then the click of the door in front of them unlocking. They headed through and up two flights of stairs until they came to number twelve, where Poole knocked on the door.

Frazer opened it wearing a blue dressing gown and checked brown slippers. His eyes were alive with panic.

"What is it?" he repeated.

"Can we come in?" Brock said levelly.

He nodded and backed away from the door and into the sitting room. As he glanced around, Poole judged that the flat was roughly the same size as his, but he guessed the rent was half the price due to the location. Knick-knacks and trinkets filled almost every available surface and ranged from small wooden carvings of stags to an ornate chessboard on a small table that looked untouched.

"Can I ask you where you were on Thursday afternoon?"

"I was at the museum," Frazer answered instantly.

"Not according to my wife," Brock said. "She said that you had taken a long lunch as you had to run some errands."

Frazer blinked rapidly before answering. "Ah, that's right, I had to run and get a few things from town."

"You were in Bexford?"

"That's right."

"You weren't near Otworth Manor?"

"No," Frazer answered. "Look, I'm really not feeling too great right now."

"Someone saw you there, Frazer," Brock said, interrupting him. "We've got a witness that can place you there."

This was stretching the truth and Brock knew it; Helen Blaxon had just seen someone with white hair and a beard, but Poole watched the effect on Frazer's face with interest.

"I wasn't there, all right?" he said as he reddened.

"We've taken the crowbar from the storeroom for analysis," Brock said.

Frazer's mouth opened, closed, and then opened again. "The crowbar? Why?"

"We're testing it to see if there is any trace evidence that it was used in the murder of Matt Pike and Clive Pentonville. Did you know either of these men?"

Frazer stepped backwards and slumped down onto his sofa. "No, no I didn't."

Poole could see what the inspector was doing. Bamboozling Frazer with a series of quick-fire questions that were designed to put him firmly outside of his comfort zone.

"And the security company," Brock continued. "They say the alarm system should have gone off at the museum?"

Frazer looked up, his face angry again. "Look, I'm not feeling well. Leave me alone and I'll talk to you later."

Brock stared at him for a moment before nodding. "OK, Frazer, but we'll be back to talk to you once we've got the lab results on this crowbar of yours."

They left Frazer, who closed the door behind them and slid a bolt across noisily as soon as he had done so.

"He's lying about something," Brock said when they stepped back out into the heat of the day. "I just don't know what. Let's get back to the station and—" Brock was cut off by his phone, which began blaring out "Copacabana" by Barry Manilow. He swore under his breath at his wife's latest ringtone selection and answered it as they began crossing the road to the car.

Brock stopped halfway and turned slowly back to the flat. "OK," he said in a sombre tone. "Thanks, Sheila." He put the phone back in his pocket and headed back towards the flats.

Poole jogged up beside him. "What's going on, sir?"

"That was Sheila," Brock answered in a low growl. "They've found traces of blood on the crowbar from the museum. Somebody had cleaned the bloody thing."

CHAPTER TWENTY-THREE

"I don't think your wife is going to be very happy with you dragging me in here," Frazer said angrily, as Brock and Poole entered the interview room at Bexford Station. "Just because someone thought they saw me at the manor house, it could have been anyone. The whole thing's ridiculous."

They took their seats and stared across at him.

They hadn't arrested him yet, but Brock had made it clear that if he didn't accompany them back to the station, he'd have to.

Frazer had grumbled but had made his way down to the car where the three of them had remained in silence until they had reached the station.

Now, Brock was ready to launch his secret weapon.

"We've found blood on the crowbar, Frazer," he said quietly. "You didn't clean it well enough."

Frazer's eyebrows knotted. "What crowbar?"

"The crowbar at the museum. The one you lent to us when we wanted to open the totem pole."

"Well, it must have got the blood on it then when you opened the pole." Frazer shrugged.

"Or it was the weapon you used to hit Matt Pike and Clive Pentonville over the head with," Brock continued.

Frazer laughed. "You can't be serious?!" He looked between the two men and his expression slowly changed. "Oh, my God. You think I had something to do with these murders?! Just because someone said they saw me up at the house?" He looked down at the plain white table between them.

"The murders occurred on Thursday, Frazer, on the grounds of Otworth Manor. Now we've got a crowbar found in your workspace, which would match the injuries sustained by the victims and has blood on it. These might be coincidences, but they don't look good all together, do they, Frazer?"

"Why would I kill them? I didn't even know them! And do you really think I'd be daft enough to bash them with a crowbar and then bring it back to the museum?!"

"Tell us where you were on Thursday."

"I told you, I was shopping."

"Which shops?"

Frazer stared back at Brock. "I was just mooching about, I can't remember all of them."

"What did you buy?"

"Nothing, I was window shopping."

"And did you see anyone you know or who might recognise you?"

"No."

Brock sighed and got up. "You're not making this easy for yourself, Frazer. You're going to have to stay here until we get the DNA back from the crowbar."

"You can't do that!"

"Actually, it's all I can do."

The inspector turned and left the room. Poole nodded at the uniformed officer who was standing in the corner of the room and followed Brock into the corridor.

"What do you think, sir?"

"What do I think? I think that I need lunch."

CHAPTER TWENTY-FOUR

"Afternoon, Sal," Brock grumbled as they entered the small sandwich shop.

Sal leaned at them from behind the counter and threw her hands wide.

"Sam! I haven't seen you since at least.... When was it? Yesterday?" She smiled mischievously. "How are you?"

"Oh, not bad," Brock grumbled.

"Ah!" Sal said, turning to Poole. "And I see that our friend is a little grumpy right now, isn't that so, Guy?"

Poole looked at Brock, who was now looking at him with one eyebrow raised, as though daring him to agree.

"We've had a difficult morning," Poole said diplomatically.

Sal laughed and shook her head, causing her black ringlets of hair to fly left and right. "No problem, you take a seat and I'll bring you something to cheer you up!" She turned and vanished through the door behind her.

"How's Laura doing?" Poole asked once they were seated at one of the two tables by the window.

"She's fine. No sickness or anything, yet," Brock answered, brightening up. "It's still early days, but it's hard not to start thinking about putting a nursery in the box bedroom."

Poole watched him smile as he looked out of the window.

"It suits you, being happy," he said, laughing.

"Well, don't get too carried away," Brock said, laughing as well. "This case isn't going to let me stay this way for long." He looked back at Poole suddenly, his eyes narrowing. "Have you thought any more about the situation with your mother?"

"Only that I'd like her to move out so I can have some space to get my head on straight."

"I thought she was going to move in with some friend of hers?"

"Yeah she was, Angela Hope she was called. I think I might have put a bit of a dampener on that by not immediately marrying her daughter Debbie."

Brock chuckled. "Ah, yeah, a certain young constable got in the way there, I'm guessing. How is the slowest-moving romance in England going?"

Poole sighed. "Slowly."

"Why?"

Poole shifted in his seat. "I don't know," he said as he fiddled with a napkin. "Maybe I'm just a bit worried that I've got too much baggage."

"Baggage?! Bloody hell." The inspector shook his large head. "Don't be stupid, Poole, it doesn't suit you."

Poole looked up at him in surprise.

"Everyone's got baggage," Brock continued. "That's how you become an adult. You accumulate baggage, good and bad, until you're a fully formed human. It doesn't make you damaged, it makes you who you are, it makes you whole."

Poole swallowed, unsure of what to say, and was saved by

Sal returning with two stacks of sandwiches, which she placed in front of them with a flourish.

"This is thin slices of steak with cheese, avocado, pickled jalapeños and a little paprika."

Brock eyed it suspiciously, as he did with everything that was new or unknown to him.

"Just try it," Sal said, rolling her dark eyes.

They both picked it up and bit into it at the same time. The explosion of smooth yet tangy flavours hit Poole at the same time as he watched Brock's face turn to one of pure enjoyment as he ate.

"You've done it again, Sal," the inspector said as he swallowed the mouthful. "That is bloody lovely."

"Ah!" she said, playfully punching him on the arm. "You are my best customer, so only the best for you!" She turned away and headed back to the counter where a small queue had begun to form.

"Did you manage to get your hands on a map of the manor?" Brock said once she'd gone.

Poole searched in his jacket pocket and pulled a folded and slightly crumpled map from it. He opened it on the table and held it open with the tomato sauce, salt and pepper, his hand holding the final corner flat.

"Here are the paths that the guests took on their horse ride. You can see how they wind all over the place, but any of them could have got back to the barn pretty sharpish if they had just gone across country here."

"Helen Blaxon said she saw Frazer near the lodge, didn't she?" Brock peered at the map, frowning.

"It's over here." Poole pointed, his finger resting by a small black square set against one of the paths that crisscrossed over the estate. "She must have been on this path.

The lodge is where Ted Daley lives. Think Frazer knows him?"

Brock looked up at him. "Why do you say that?"

"I just wondered, I mean, Frazer must have been there for a reason, right? And they're similar ages, they could be friends." He shrugged.

Brock looked thoughtful for a moment and then got up. "I'll get this and a couple of coffees to go, why don't you call your dad?"

Poole looked up at him. "And ask about Matt Pike?"

"Yes, and make sure that he knows not to tell your mum that the attack on your house might have been partly her fault."

"They don't talk," Poole said blankly.

"Ah, but who knows what's going to happen now your dad's around here?" Brock turned off towards the counter, leaving Poole to pull his phone out and stare at it.

He had spent the last few weeks trying to keep all of this at bay. He hadn't wanted to face the fact his mother could have been involved in the death of his friend, in him getting shot. Now he had faced up to that conversation, and everything still felt just as unfinished as it had done before.

Did he blame both his mother and father? Yes, there was no denying that. But could he blame both of them forever, knowing that the other was equally responsible? His father may have been breaking the law, knowingly or not, but he must surely have never anticipated the sudden violence that had come to their door?

His mother had thought she was doing the right thing by trying to get his father out of the whole business, but instead, she had brought a fiery revenge upon their family and his friends.

Or was he now just making excuses for them because, secretly, he wanted them both in his life?

He looked up and saw that Brock was approaching the front of the queue. He got up and walked outside.

"Guy! How are you?" his dad's voice came down the line. Poole leaned back against the exterior wall of Sal's and squinted in the sun.

"I'm fine. I talked to Mum."

"Oh, I'm sorry. What happened?"

"I didn't tell her that she might have been responsible for the attack."

There was a slight pause and Poole thought he detected the faint sound of a sigh. Was that relief?

"Well done, son," his father's voice came down the line. "What did you say?"

Poole wondered about this unexpected praise but continued, anyway. "I just told her that I knew she'd tried to get you out of it all, and I don't want you to say anything else to her or anyone else."

"I haven't spoken about this with her for ten years, do you think I'm going to now?"

His father had spoken in a light, amused tone, but there was something behind his voice that made Poole wonder how bitter he was about his mother's intervention. After all, it had sent him to jail and lost him his son.

"I have a case and wondered if you could help."

"Happy to," came the immediate reply. "If I can, obviously."

"A man's been murdered; apparently he's known to move high-end stolen goods. His name's Matt Pike. I was wondering if you knew him?"

"Never heard of him," Jack answered.

"Do you think you could ask around? See if anyone you know might have known him?"

"I'll see what I can do," Jack said brightly. "I'd like to see you again, Guy. Just to talk."

Poole pushed himself off the wall as Brock appeared from the door of Sal's holding two coffees. "I've got a lot going on right now," Poole said hurriedly into the phone. "Maybe in a week or so."

"Great," Jack answered. "I'll get back to you on this Pike chap."

The line went dead and Poole placed the phone back in his pocket as he took his coffee from the inspector.

"Well?" Brock asked.

"He'd never heard of Matt Pike, but he's looking into it."

"That's not what I bloody meant and you know it," Brock grumbled.

Poole took a sip of his coffee and immediately regretted it as it burned his lips and mouth. "He seemed glad that I hadn't told Mum everything," Poole said as he wiped his mouth on the sleeve of his jacket.

Brock nodded thoughtfully. "Come on then, we need to get back out to the manor house."

CHAPTER TWENTY-FIVE

They found Lucy Flowers in the small office that was set into the stable block at one end. She was leaning over her desk with a pair of reading glasses perched on the end of her nose as Poole opened the door.

"Oh," she said, looking up at them with a concerned expression. "I'm afraid I'm rather busy at the moment."

"This won't take long, Mrs Flowers," Poole said, as they moved in front of the desk. There was only one chair and so Poole decided to stand next to it. Brock didn't sit either, instead choosing to lean on the back of the chair as he stared at Lucy Flowers.

"Show her the photo, Poole," he said.

"Oh, right." Poole fumbled the photo of Frazer Mullins loose from his pocket and held it in front of Lucy. "Do you recognise this man?"

"No, I don't," Lucy said immediately. She looked back down at her desk and began flicking through the papers in front of her again.

Brock looked at Poole and raised an eyebrow. "Can you

look again, Mrs Flowers? This man is a suspect in a murder inquiry."

Lucy's head jerked up. "A murder inquiry?"

"Yes, you do remember that someone was murdered in the totem pole donated by this estate?"

"Yes, but I—" Her eyes flickered for a moment. "I'm sorry, I've never seen that man in my life. Now you must excuse me, I have a lot to get through."

Poole waited for the inevitable explosion of anger from the inspector, but it didn't come. Instead, he hesitated, staring at the top of Lucy Flowers' head, which was still bowed to the work in front of her, before he turned and left.

"She seemed a bit evasive," Poole said when they were outside.

"She's bloody lying," Brock answered flatly.

"About knowing Frazer?"

"Who knows, but there's something there, something she doesn't want to talk to us about. Let's see what Ted Daley's got to say for himself."

They walked through the stable yard, admiring the horses who leaned out from their stalls and chewed on the hay which was in a basket on the wall next to each stall. A girl was scraping the yard with a shovel, shattering the peace of the afternoon.

"Poole," Brock said, gesturing to the girl. "Go and ask her if she's seen Frazer."

Poole headed over to the girl, who stopped working as he approached. She looked up at him, squinting in the early afternoon sunshine.

"Excuse me, but do you recognise this man?" He held the picture out in front of him.

"Are you from the police or something?" she said, smiling.

"Yes, can you look at the picture please?"

"Ooh! Is this about that murder?!"

"Can you just look at the picture please?" Poole asked, trying not to become exasperated.

The girl leaned in, squinting at the photo. "Oh him, yeah he's round all the time."

Poole stared at her in shock. "This man? Are you sure?" He turned back to Brock, who was now motoring towards them.

"Yeah, he's always around here. I've seen him with Mrs Flowers before, you should ask her."

Poole turned back towards the office where through the plate-glass front he could see Lucy Flowers staring at them, the colour draining from her face.

"Come on," Brock said, heading towards her.

Poole followed, ignoring the shout of the girl from behind him who called, "Am I an important witness? Do you think the TV will want to talk to me?"

"That girl says you've met with this man regularly here, Mrs Flowers," Brock bellowed as they entered the office. "So, I'd like to know why you felt the need to lie to a police officer in the middle of a murder investigation?"

"I'm not saying anything until I speak to a lawyer," she said, her voice shaking.

CHAPTER TWENTY-SIX

"Damn," Brock said angrily.

Poole followed his gaze and saw Ted Daley sitting atop a large ride-on lawn mower. He was parked and staring across towards the stables where the presence of two police cars stuck out like a sore thumb.

"You didn't want him to see us taking Mrs Flowers into custody?"

"Not before we'd spoken to him, no. Oh well, come on." Brock walked down the side of the stable block and waved a hand at Ted in the distance. He raised a hand back and began to drive slowly over to them, the ride-on lawnmower chugging along beneath him.

"Everything OK, Inspector?" he said as pulled he up in front of them and killed the engine with a turn of the key.

"We're taking Mrs Flowers into the station to answer a few questions." Brock turned to Poole and gestured to him to show Ted the picture. "Do you know this man?" Brock asked as Poole held it out.

Ted licked his lips as he looked at the photo. "I think I've seen him before, why?"

"Well, that's a better answer than Mrs Flowers gave," Brock said, studying the leathery face of the man in front of him.

"How do you mean?" Ted said warily.

Brock narrowed his eyes. "She told us she'd never seen the man before, then a witness told us that she'd seen Mrs Flowers talking to this gentleman regularly."

"I wouldn't know about that," Ted said, looking decidedly uncomfortable at the whole conversation. "I'd better be getting on, anyway."

"Don't you want to know what the man in the photo's done?" Brock asked.

Ted blinked rapidly. "All right, what's he done?"

"He's being questioned about the recent murders."

"What? You think he's got something to do with Clive being killed?! And that other man?!"

"Why does that surprise you, Mr Daley?" Brock asked, folding his arms.

"It doesn't, just an unpleasant business, that's all."

"Do you know, I think it might be of some use to our investigation if you joined Mrs Flowers down at the station, Mr Daley."

"What? Why?!"

"Because, like her, I think you're lying to me."

Ted Daley raised his chin but said nothing.

Brock sighed and waved him off the mower. "Come on then. If you're going to be an obstinate bugger, then you might as well do it back at the station as here."

"MRS FLOWERS, SHALL WE START AGAIN?" Brock said, sliding the picture of Frazer across the small table towards her. "Do you know this man?"

"Yes, it's Frazer Mullins."

"And how do you know him?"

"He likes horses, he visits the stables sometimes."

"And why did you lie to us and say that you had never seen him before?"

"I was in shock, you had told me that he might be connected to the murders and I just panicked."

Poole noticed Brock's eyes flick between Lucy Flowers and her lawyer, a woman in a light grey suit with intelligent eyes. She had done a good job of preparing her client.

"We have Ted Daley in for questioning too, Mrs Flowers," Brock said.

"Ted? He's nothing to do with this."

"Nothing to do with what, Mrs Flowers?"

Lucy's mouth fell open slightly as she turned to her lawyer with a panicked look in her eye.

"I think it might be best if I had another moment with my client," the lawyer said, her lips pursed.

"Very well," Brock said, standing. "We'll give you some time, but I suggest you think through what you want to do here very carefully."

"What do you think, sir?" Poole said as they stepped out of the room and back into the corridor.

"I think we go and talk to Ted Daley now," he said, heading down the corridor to the interview room where the odd-job man had been installed.

Ted Daley was nursing a cup of tea and talking to Constable Davies when they entered the room. He looked up at them but turned back to Davies to finish his sentence before addressing them.

"You want to pinch the tip off of the main shoot above the fourth leaf truss," he finished.

"Right, thanks," Davies said, his cheeks reddening as he looked up at Brock's questioning face. "Mr Daley was giving me some advice about my mum's tomato plants. She's having a bit of trouble and I thought Mr Daley might know..."

"All right, all right!" Brock said, silencing Davies with a wave of his hand.

They took their seats in the chairs opposite Ted Daley as Davies scurried back to his corner and stood to attention, eyes forward.

"Mr Daley, now that the gardening chat is out of the way, perhaps we can get some answers from you on how you know Frazer Mullins?"

"I don't know him." Ted shrugged. "That's the man in the photo's name, is it?" he said, picking up the picture that Poole had laid in front of him. "I think you're best off talking to Lucy about him."

"And why's that?"

"I've seen 'em together a fair bit on the estate." He looked up at Brock and frowned.

"What is it?" the inspector asked, sensing there was information buried behind the tanned, leathery face of the man in front of him.

"I know why you've brought me down here, it's because you think there's something fishy going on with Lucy and this Frazer chap. Am I right?"

Brock thought for a moment before answering. "You're right, and I guess you've been thinking something similar to jump to that conclusion?"

"I have." Ted nodded, stone-faced. "I've seen them together on the estate, and every time they see me coming, they get out of sight sharpish. I always thought that it was

Lucy's boyfriend or something, though she's never mentioned one. I try to stay out of other people's business, but there was something shifty about those two." He looked off into the distance as though dredging through memories.

"How many times have you seen him on the estate?"

"Oh, quite a bit. I thought he had a horse at the stables at first," he smiled, "then I realised it wasn't the horses he was interested in."

"And did you see him on the estate on Thursday?"

"Nope, Thursday's my day off. I spent it in the garden weeding."

"Anyone that can vouch for that?"

"Nope, just me."

"OK, well, you should be able to go home in a short while, if you don't mind just being patient for a little longer."

"No problem." Ted nodded, and sipped at his tea.

CHAPTER TWENTY-SEVEN

A few minutes later, Brock and Poole were standing in front of the battered coffee machine in Bexford Police Station's canteen.

"So we've got Lucy Flowers deciding whether she wants to fill us in on whatever's going on between her and Frazer. I mean, Ted Daley's pretty much confirmed there's something funny going on, but he doesn't seem to know what it is."

Brock's coffee cup was full, and he moved it away from the machine to add sugar.

"I think it's time we checked this the other way around, don't you?" he said brightly.

"The other way around?" Poole said as he moved his cup under the stained spout of the coffee machine.

"Frazer's still here, waiting. Why don't we go and tell him we've got Mrs Flowers and Mr Daley in custody and see what he makes of the news, eh? He might just wonder what they've said about him..." Brock left the thought hanging.

Poole grinned. "I like that."

"I thought you might." Brock chuckled. They headed

towards the door to the main room of the station as Anderson burst through with a look of thunder on his face. He caught sight of them and his eyes seemed to linger on Brock's as his scowl deepened.

"Sir," he said, spitting the word out as though it was poison.

"Anderson," Brock said in an even tone before moving through the door.

Poole held back and headed over to Anderson, who was now at the coffee machine himself.

"What's your problem, Anderson?"

Anderson's large frame swivelled towards him. "My problem is that your bloody boss is trying his best to wreck things around here. Messing with the way things should be."

"What on earth are you talking about?" Poole asked, mystified.

Anderson leaned over him until Poole could feel the heat of his breath on his face. "Your bloody boss is going for the chief inspector's job when he knows it should go to Sharp."

Poole felt a pang of panic. The idea of Brock moving up the food chain and away from him was not one he had planned for. When the inspector had mentioned the possibility the other day, he had pushed it to the back of his mind, not wanting to contemplate it. Now it appeared he would have to.

"Sharp would be just as useless as Tannock is. We don't need another chief inspector on the golf course," he snapped, as a sudden wave of anger took him over.

As soon as the words had left his lips, he knew he had made a mistake. He watched the corner of Anderson's lip curl in a smirk, his eyes alive with mischief. He was about to turn away and get the hell out of there when he saw

Anderson's eyes flicker to his left before his expression spread into a wide grin.

"Pond, isn't it?" a voice said from behind him.

He turned to see Detective Inspector Sharp standing with his hands behind his back. His moustache bristled as he looked down his large nose at Poole, who was staring at him with wide eyes.

"It's Poole, sir," he managed despite his throat closing.

"Right, well, I'll be sure to remember that for the future, eh?" Sharp rocked on his heels, his hands together behind his back, and eyed Poole like a bug to be stepped on.

"Poole?" Brock's voice came from the doorway.

"Coming, sir!" Poole called back, relief rushing through him as he hurried away.

"What was going on there?" Brock asked as they headed back down the corridor.

"Are you taking the chief inspector's job?"

Brock stopped in his tracks and stared at Poole, who slowed and turned back to him.

"Who did you hear that from?"

"Anderson."

Brock nodded, his nostrils flaring slightly. "He said that, did he indeed? Well, I haven't made any decisions yet, I told you the other day. I've just been asked to apply."

"Right."

They hovered awkwardly for a moment before Brock cleared his throat loudly and headed off again. Poole followed him, his mind racing. The situation with his mother had made him feel more alone than ever. In the few months he had known Brock, he had become a friend, maybe even like family. The thought of not working with him anymore was bringing the anxieties he initially had about his job here rushing back.

He took a deep breath as they reached the holding cell where Frazer Mullins was being kept and tried to clear his head.

"Frazer," Brock said as they were let into the cramped cell by the custody sergeant. "It seems we have a couple of your friends here at the station."

"Friends?" Frazer said, looking up from the small bed he was sitting on.

"Lucy Flowers and Ted Daley. They've both been very helpful."

Frazer's eyes darted around the room before returning to Brock's. "Why have you brought them in?"

"Because we think you and Lucy are up to your necks in it, and we take murder cases very seriously."

"No! Lucy and I had nothing to do with that! We would never have hurt anybody!"

"Really?" Brock said with surprise. "Even if they discovered what you were up to with all your little trips to the manor?"

"Look," Frazer said, leaning forward. His elbows rested on the table in front of him, his eyes pleading, desperate. "We were just trying to get a little bit of money together; they had more than enough at that bloody manor."

Poole tried not to let the surprise show on his face. He was fairly certain the inspector had been hoping to provoke Frazer with the possible affair that Ted Daley had guessed might be occurring between Lucy Flowers and the Scottish museum worker. This, though; this sounded like something else. Poole realised that Brock had come to the same conclusion.

"So what happened? Did someone find out what you were up to and you decided to silence them?"

"No! I'd never hurt anyone." He shook his head slowly in disbelief at the situation in which he had found himself.

"If not you, then maybe we need to go and talk to Mrs Flowers more about this?"

Frazer looked up in terror. "No, Lucy had nothing to do with those deaths, neither of us did!"

"I think you'd better tell me everything, don't you? That way, we might just believe you regarding the murder."

"Lucy and I met about a year ago," Frazer said quietly, his eyes fixed and unseeing on the desk in front of him. "She was at the museum and I near-enough knocked off her feet coming out of the storeroom. I made her a cup of tea to say sorry and we got talking." He looked up, his eyes suddenly fierce. "Her husband's a mean bastard, make no mistake. It's him you should have locked away in here, not me or Lucy."

"You and Lucy are having an affair?" Poole asked.

"Don't make it sound sordid, young man," Frazer bristled. "Lucy married young and her husband turned out to be a monster. She and I found each other, but she couldn't just leave him."

"Why not?"

"You don't understand what he's like." Frazer laughed mirthlessly. "The man's psychotic. Lucy's tried to leave him lots of times. He always tracks her down, he always finds her. There's only one way we could get away from him properly, and that's with money."

"So you decided to steal from the estate?" Brock asked.

"That stuff had been in there for years, no one even knows what half of it is! We just wanted to take a few bits that would let us get away somewhere and start again, far enough away that he couldn't find us."

"And were you selling these bits to someone called Matt Pike?" Brock asked.

Frazer frowned. "What? No, I sold them on eBay. Whatever happened to that bloke, it was nothing to do with Lucy and me."

"You're telling me you'd never heard the name Matt Pike before he ended up dead?"

"No! Of course, I haven't!" Poole watched him take a deep breath, trying to calm himself. "Look, whatever these murders are about, they're nothing to do with what we were doing." He looked up at them, his arms folded.

"So you would go to the estate, meet Lucy, and the two of you would find some small items you could sell that you hoped wouldn't be missed?" Poole said.

"That's right."

"You were there on Thursday, though," Poole continued. "So why were you at the estate when it was Lucy's day off?"

"I wasn't! Whoever told you that was a liar, or they mistook someone else for me!"

"And what about the break-in?" Brock asked. "There's something you're not telling us there. What was it? Did you and Lucy decide to step up your game and steal something from the museum as well?"

"No!"

"Is that why you called in sick after that body had been found? Did you think you were going to get the blame for it?"

"Look, Lucy and I were nothing to do with the break-in, but whoever it was didn't get stuck at the door, they got all the way in."

"You mean they did get into the museum?" Poole asked in surprise.

Frazer nodded. "I didn't want to admit it, but I forgot to set the alarm. Truth is, I like to have a drink of an evening."

Brock coughed.

"OK, of an afternoon, then," Frazer continued, looking at

him. "I forget to set the alarm sometimes. It's never been a problem before, there's nothing of real value in there."

"But someone broke in on Thursday night and made it into the museum," Brock said slowly, his mind clearly turning over the possibilities of this. "And you have no idea who it could have been?"

Frazer shook his head.

CHAPTER TWENTY-EIGHT

Brock and Poole were sitting in the canteen of the station with Constables Sanders and Davies, all of them in a forlorn mood.

"If someone broke into the museum," Sanita said, looking at Poole, "then it means that the murder could have been committed there after all?"

"Maybe," Poole said, shrugging.

"Which means you're back to square one in terms of finding someone who did it?"

"Not back to square one, Sanders," Brock said irritably. "We're back to suspecting everyone who works at the museum."

Sanita looked from the inspector to Poole and then back again. "Surely sir, you don't think Laura...?"

"Of course I bloody don't!" Brock snapped. "But she's going to be right in the thick of it again, now, until we can actually catch a break here."

"I think it's one of that lot back at the manor house,"

Davies said after an awkward silence. "I didn't like the look of any of that lot."

"Right bloody rude they were to me, an' all," Sanita added.

Poole watched the inspector's face, but it remained unchanged for the deep scowl that was etched into his large features.

They had gone from their conversation with Frazer, straight to Lucy Flowers, who had confirmed Frazer's version of events, and denied any knowledge of the museum break-in.

Worse than this was that both Brock and Poole believed them. This was what had left them all in a sombre mood and now, as Brock had said, Laura might be caught up in it again.

Brock took a deep breath and leaned backwards. "Sanders, Davies, I want you both to look into Frazer's eBay account and check what he's sold and how much for.

"I want him and Lucy Flowers charged with theft even if they didn't have anything to do with the murders. Besides, we can see if that will jog their memory about any other details they might have conveniently forgotten."

The two constables left, with Sanita giving Poole a small, sympathetic smile as she did so. Poole returned the gesture but felt a pang of guilt at how little he had spoken to her over the last couple of days.

"I don't think any of the three we've got in here did it, Poole," Brock said, fixing his gaze with his grey eyes. "And I can't see any reason for someone to have broken into the museum and not stolen anything, unless something went wrong and they killed their partner while they were there."

"But Clive Pentonville was found at the estate," Poole said. "If we're saying the same person killed them both, then it doesn't make any sense that one of them would have been killed at the museum and one at the manor house."

"Unless they were killed by different people?" Brock said with a faraway look in his eye.

Poole blinked in confusion. "But there can't be two killers, surely. The cases are too wrapped up in each other. We know Clive Pentonville went to school with Matt Pike, and Clive tried to buy the totem pole from the museum before it had even got there."

"Before it had got there," Brock repeated, his eyes suddenly coming alive. "What if Clive Pentonville wasn't trying to buy the pole to get the Shakespeare folio, but because he knew the body of Matt Pike was in there?"

"You mean he tried to buy it from the museum to stop it getting there and being discovered?"

"Exactly, which would mean he either killed Matt Pike himself, or he knew who did and wanted to protect them."

"His brother!" Poole said excitedly. "It has to be his brother. He didn't like any of his brother's friends, and I can't see him being willing to cover up a murder for any of them."

Brock nodded. "I think we need to have another word with Simon Pentonville, and maybe this time we'll make it more formal. It can wait until tomorrow though. We should have the results from the blood on the crowbar from the museum by then, and who knows what that's going to bloody say."

CHAPTER TWENTY-NINE

"How are my favourite two people?" Brock said, as he came through the door and Laura and their dog Indy came to greet him.

"Oh, bloody hell, are you referring to Indy as 'people' now?" Laura said, rolling her eyes.

"I didn't mean Indy, did I, fella?" Brock said, bending and rubbing the scruff at the top of the dog's head. "I meant the new member of the household." He got up and placed his hand on Laura's stomach. They smiled at each other, both glowing in the pure joy of it all.

"So Indy's been relegated to third place in your affections already, has he?"

"Third place?" Brock said with a twinkle in his eye. "You think you're above him, do you?"

Laura punched him in the arm, laughing, and headed off to the kitchen.

"Any luck on the case?"

"Actually, there's something I need to tell you," he said, his voice now serious.

She stopped and turned back to him from the kitchen doorway. "What is it? Is it something to do with Frazer?"

Brock nodded and moved towards her, took her arm and led her to a stool by the breakfast bar while he grabbed a bottle of red wine from the rack and began opening it.

"He's been stealing from the Otworth Estate, taking things from the collection in the barn there."

"What?! No, he can't have!"

"Afraid so, confessed to it himself. Only smaller things, I think. I think you should do an inventory check, though, just in case he decided to help himself to some things from the museum as well."

"I just can't believe it," Laura said, shaking her head again. "He must have needed the money badly," she said, turning to Brock. "He wouldn't have done it otherwise, he's just not that sort."

"If there's one thing I've learnt in doing this job, it's that given the right circumstances, everyone's the sort."

"Wait a minute," she said, eyes wide. "You don't still think he had anything to do with these murders, do you?" She clasped her hands to her mouth. "You do, don't you? You think he killed them to cover up his crimes!"

"Bloody hell, Laura, let's not get carried away, eh? No, I don't think he was involved in the murders, but I can't rule him out."

She stared at him for a moment with a fire in her eyes, but it died in front of him and she nodded. He moved towards her and took her in his arms.

"I'll get to the bottom of this and then everything will be back to normal."

She smiled at him. "Except for the obvious," she said, her hands moving to her stomach. "Oh!" she said suddenly. "And what about this promotion? Have you thought about it anymore?"

"No, not really." He took a seat on one of the stools. "Poole knows."

He had attempted to say this with nonchalance, but there had been a strain in his voice that was unmistakable to Laura.

"I take it he wasn't all that happy at the idea of you leaving him."

"Leaving him? We're not bloody married."

"Oh, come on, you know what I mean."

"He seemed a bit put out, yes," Brock agreed. He moved away from her, rubbing his face with his hands, and poured two glasses of wine. He slid one towards Laura.

"Really?" she said, raising her eyebrows and sliding it back.

"Oh, right," he said, smiling.

CHAPTER THIRTY

Poole pulled the door key from his pocket and then paused, his hand halfway to the keyhole.

He imagined his mother on the other side of the door. Would she be waiting for him, ready to continue their conversation of that morning? He wasn't sure he could handle that, but he was tired. He'd have to face the music.

He pushed the key into the lock and opened the door. He realised with a rush of relief that there was no familiar drone of the TV, and his mother wasn't in her usual position, sprawled on the sofa.

He exhaled slowly in relief and closed the door behind him. She was obviously out, which would hopefully mean he had enough time to make some food and disappear into his room before she came back.

He moved to the kitchen and saw a sheet of notepaper on the work surface.

"Guy,

I've gone to stay with Angela.
Mum"

He felt his entire body sag with relief, but there was only a moment of this before guilt rushed in.

His mother had seen how upset he had been. He might not have revealed her real role in what had happened to their family, but she had clearly seen enough to know that he blamed her.

He closed his eyes and swore to the empty room before grabbing a beer from the fridge and leaning on the counter.

He thought about messaging her and picked up his phone to do so, when he saw a message from Sanita. It must have come in while he drove home.

He opened it.

"Do you fancy going for a quick drink tonight? I thought you could come by the restaurant?"

He blinked and read the message again to make sure he wasn't seeing things. Sanita wanted him to come to her family's restaurant? Bloody hell. She must want him to meet them.

He gulped at the beer in his hand and tried to breathe slowly, but his heart was hammering in his chest.

He felt as though he had ignored Sanita for days, barely speaking to her at work and only replying to the two messages she had sent with belated, curt replies.

He drank again. He had begun to push her away, just like he knew he would. He cast his mind back to earlier when he had been sitting in Sal's with the inspector. What was it he had said? That everyone had baggage they had accumulated through life, and that was what made you *you*.

He downed the rest of his beer and picked up the phone.

Maybe it was time he started moving on from what had happened to him. He wore the scars, yes, but he was alive. Unlike poor Simon who had died that night, he had a life to lead.

CHAPTER THIRTY-ONE

Poole wiped his hands on his jeans for the fourth time. The night was clammy and his nerves had sent his body into a nervous sweat, which made the shirt he wore cling to his back.

He saw the sign for the Balti Towers restaurant, which hung from an ornate iron post on the side of the small white building. It was old, with narrow, crooked windows at the end of a row of terraced houses. All of which had been converted to house-independent shops selling various niche items. Poole rolled his eyes when he passed a health food shop that his mother had recommended to him multiple times.

Poole arrived at the door of the restaurant and reached for the handle, deciding that if he stopped, he might lose the courage to go in at all.

"Good evening, sir," a good-looking man in his early twenties said as the door swung open before Poole could touch it. "A table for one, is it? Or are you meeting somebody?" The man had the same northern twang to his voice, and Poole wondered if he was family.

"Um, actually, I was looking for Sanita?"

The man's smile fell and a sharp frown line jutted down his forehead.

"You're looking for Sanita? And why would you be looking for her?"

"We were going to have a drink?" Poole said slightly feebly.

He was regretting coming; he wasn't in the right frame of mind to be harangued by northern men with a hard look in their eye.

"Give it a rest, Parv," Sanita's voice came from inside the restaurant to the left.

She appeared through the side door, shoving Parv in the chest as she did so.

"Guy, this is my brother, Parv. He's an idiot."

Parv snorted but gave Poole a nod.

"Hi," Poole managed, still a little dazed by the introduction.

"Come on," Sanita said. "My mum's out the back and she's desperate to say hello." She took Poole's hand and led him through the restaurant.

Tables were packed into the small, square room, leaving the occupants with their elbows almost touching those on the next table. It was busy, and the chatter of the various people who were either tucking into their meals or waiting with drinks gave the place a vibrant feel.

Sanita weaved through the tables, pulling Poole along behind her until they passed the bar at the back of the room and stepped through a swing door into a hot and noisy kitchen.

A woman was standing with their back to them, barking

orders in a loud voice at two men and one woman who rushed about the shining metal surfaces with various pots, pans and ladles.

"Mum?" Sanita said when the woman had finished her barrage. "Guy's here."

The woman turned and Poole instantly saw the likeness of Sanita in her eyes, which were dark and ever so slightly mischievous. She pulled a pair of glasses from where they had been hidden in her tied-back grey hair and put them on the end of her nose.

"This is him, is it?" she said, moving forward and clasping Poole with a hand on each shoulder. She stared at him for a moment before nodding. "He has a kind face, and he is tall."

"Guy, this is my mother Karun."

"Nice to meet you," Guy managed.

"We thought we'd grab a drink at the bar if you can join us for a bit?" Sanita said, smiling.

Her mother moved across to a shelf where several orders lay skewered on spikes. Her finger moved across them as she moved down the line. "OK, I can spare ten minutes," she said, before heading out through the door they'd come through.

Sanita grinned at Poole and headed after her. He noticed the back door and for a moment considered making a run for it, before sighing and heading back through to the restaurant.

"Guy, I want to know all about you," Karun said, grabbing two stools while Sanita ordered them drinks. "Tell me about your parents."

Poole's mouth hung open and gaped there like a fish who had just found the surrounding sea had vanished.

"My parents?"

"Oh! His mum, Jenny's lovely," Sanita said over his shoulder. "You'd like her, Mum."

"Then I will have to meet her!" Karun said. "Guy here

seems shy, so I will have to talk to the mother. And what about your father, what is his name?"

"Jack," Poole said in a hollow voice.

"Jack," repeated Karun, nodding. She took the drink offered to her by her daughter, a tall gin and tonic, and sipped at it. "And what does Jack do?"

Poole's mouth opened and closed again when his phone buzzed in his pocket. He hastily retrieved it, glad of the interruption, and was thrown as he looked at the screen and saw his father's name there.

"This is my dad now, I'm sorry, but I better answer it."

"Of course!" Karun said, standing up. "Family is important. I wish my Sanita would return my calls," she said, waving her arms.

"Oh, come on Mum, you have me helping out here at least twice a week, I think we see enough of each other!"

Poole turned away and answered as he made his way back through the restaurant and out onto the street.

"Hello?"

"Guy, it's your dad. I've got some information on this Matt Pike of yours."

"OK, what is it?"

"I reached out to a few people, but no one had heard of him. Then an associate of mine overheard me talking on the phone and said they'd met him."

Poole's mind hung on the phrase "an associate." There was something in that phrase that conjured the criminal class, and he wondered where exactly his dad had been when he'd been overheard.

"He said he'd met him here in Bexford because this Matt Pike was looking for some hired help," Jack Poole continued.

"What do you mean 'hired help'?"

"He was looking for someone to beat the crap out of somebody else," his father said drily.

Poole looked back through the restaurant window towards Sanita at the bar. His father had been gone from his life for so long that the memory of him from before had become fuzzy, but he was sure he hadn't spoken like this before. Hadn't acted like this before.

Poole remembered him as a fun, mild-mannered man that you would picture working in a post office rather than robbing one. Now, though, he seemed different, and more like the gangster the papers had made him out to be when he had been arrested.

"Who was he trying to get beaten up and why?"

"I can't tell you why, but I can tell you who. Some chap called Simon Pentonville. Apparently, he was looking for someone to help relieve him of something."

"Matt Pike wanted someone to help rob Simon Pentonville?"

"That's about the size of it, yes."

"And who was this acquaintance of yours?"

"You know I can't tell you that, Guy."

"You have to," Poole said angrily. "This man might have been the person who killed Clive Pentonville, he could be a murderer!"

"Not this chap," his father answered calmly. "He was supposed to meet Matt Pike on Thursday evening where they'd stage a mugging and he'd take some book off the Pentonville bloke. Neither of them showed up."

"A book, did you say?"

"Yeah, that's what he said. He thought it was a bit strange, but there it is."

"I'm still going to need the name of who told you this."

There was a pause on the other end of the line before his

father answered. "See where you get with what I told you. If you really need it, then call me again."

The line went dead and Poole looked up to see Sanita appear in the doorway of the restaurant.

"Is everything OK?" she said, concern etched on her face.

"It's the case, I think we might have a break."

"You'd better call Brock then," she said matter-of-factly, her hands on her hips.

"Right, yes," Poole said awkwardly. "Can you tell your mum I'll just be a minute?"

"She's gone back to the kitchen." Sanita waved her hand dismissively. "Anyway, it looks like it's going to be a busy night tonight because of the Sunday special we're running, so I might help out while I'm here. You go on and do what you need to, I'll see you tomorrow."

She moved towards him, pecked him on the cheek and disappeared back into the restaurant before Poole could even answer. He saw Sanita's brother Parv scowling at him from the doorway and so turned back towards his flat and called Brock, explaining the call from his father.

"We need to get over to the manor house and talk to Simon Pentonville. He made out that he could barely remember Matt Pike, that he hadn't seen him since his brother was at school with him. He was lying through his bloody teeth," Brock growled down the phone.

"Right, sir, shall I pick you up from your house?"

"Yes, but not now. If Simon Pentonville is behind this, he doesn't have a clue we're onto him. It can wait until morning. See you tomorrow, Poole."

Poole said goodbye and pushed the phone back in his pocket. He turned back towards the restaurant and hesitated for a moment, unsure of what to do.

He knew he should go back. Sanita had asked him there,

she had wanted him to meet her family. It was a big deal. He turned away and began walking, telling himself that the restaurant was busy and Sanita would be helping out anyway, but he knew he was really just avoiding more questions about his parents.

He continued strolling through the moonlit streets of Bexford. It really was a beautiful town. The butter-coloured stone of the buildings gave it a warm and inviting feel even at night. As he turned down a side street, a shortcut back to his flat, he became aware of footsteps echoing around the narrow street behind him. He turned to see a tall, broad figure in a coat with the collar turned up, which covered the person's face in shadow.

A chill ran through him and he spun back to the way he was headed and picked up his pace.

He frowned at his own jumpiness. Why was he so on edge? He thought of the man he had seen standing near his flat the other night and wondered.

As he reached the end of the side street, he suddenly sped up his walk and darted around the right-hand corner. He broke into a run and dived behind a skip that was outside of a terraced house. He had seen it yesterday and had known it would be there.

He waited for a few moments until the figure emerged from the side street. He watched them stop and look up and down the street.

They were looking for him.

He got up as they turned their head in his direction again. "I see you!" he shouted, his mouth open before he had thought of what to say.

The figure turned and ran in the opposite direction, leaving Poole leaning on the skip, his heart thumping in his chest.

CHAPTER THIRTY-TWO

"Morning, Poole," Brock said, as he climbed into the beaten Mondeo Poole drove. The car's suspension sank to the left as it took his weight.

"Morning, sir," Poole said.

"Laura insisted on making me breakfast this morning, so we're going to have to call in at Sal's on the way."

Poole smiled. Laura Brock was known for her terrible cooking, which was why the inspector took every opportunity to eat either at the station or Sal's.

"What's the matter with you?" Brock said as they pulled away.

Poole looked across and saw that he was staring at him curiously.

"You look like you've been up half the night."

"I didn't sleep well," Poole answered.

"Come on, then, let's have it," Brock said, clearly not about to let it go.

"I'm just being silly, I'm sure, but last night I thought someone was following me."

"Following you?" Brock said, alarmed.

Poole recounted the events of the previous night and waited for Brock to respond. The inspector pulled a packet of cigarettes from his pocket, opened the window a crack, and lit one.

"And you didn't see their face at all?"

"No, but I'm pretty sure it was a man. He was pretty tall and broad. I thought I saw someone watching me the other day as well, outside Byron Lanister's place."

"You didn't mention it."

"I didn't think much of it at the time."

Brock took another drag on the cigarette. "Do you think this has something to do with your dad?"

Poole's hands gripped the wheel more tightly, turning his knuckles white. "I don't know," he said quietly. "Maybe."

"We need to put someone on your flat."

"No, I'm fine, thanks, sir."

"Poole, it's not just you I'm thinking of, it's your mother."

"She's not at mine right now, she's staying with a friend."

"Oh, that's something at least," Brock said as he flicked the remaining stub of his cigarette out of the window. "Can you think of a reason your dad would have you followed?"

"No. Unless he thought he was looking out for me for some reason?"

"There's only one way to find out," Brock said. "Call him."

Poole nodded but said nothing.

If he was honest with himself, he was sure that whoever had followed him last night was not there for his protection.

CHAPTER THIRTY-THREE

"Bloody hell, do you know what time it is?!" Simon Pentonville said, as he opened the door of Otworth Manor.

"I can tell you exactly what time it is, Mr Pentonville," Brock said, pushing past him and moving into the large hallway. "It's time you started giving us the truth."

"What are you talking about?" Simon snapped, wheeling around to face him.

"You told us you hadn't seen Matt Pike since he was at school with your brother, but that wasn't true, was it?"

Simon's face looked as though it had been struck.

"You met him recently, didn't you?" Brock continued.

"I just said I remembered him from Clive's school days, I never said I hadn't seen him recently." Simon spoke slowly, as though he was working out the sentence as he went along.

"You contacted him because you thought you'd found out where the Shakespeare folio was."

Simon swallowed, his face paling. He turned to his left as Ellie Kendall emerged from the dining room.

"What's going on, Simon?" Ellie said in the amused voice she always seemed to have.

"Nothing. Go back into the dining room," Simon snapped. He marched towards the study they had been in on their previous visit. "We can talk in here," he muttered to Brock and Poole. They followed him, leaving a startled Ellie scurrying back to the dining room.

Simon Pentonville was sitting in the chair on the far side of the desk and put his hands together against his lips as though he were praying.

Brock and Poole took the two seats facing him and waited for him to speak.

"OK, I'll be straight with you," he said quietly. "But you need to hear me out."

"We will," Brock grunted.

"I knew the folio was real, we both did."

"You and your brother?"

"Yes. Our father used to taunt us with it." He gazed past them now, his mind in the past. "He never actually mentioned it of course, but he always let us know that we weren't going to get our hands on the only valuable thing of his poxy estate."

Poole gave an involuntary snort and Simon looked at him sharply.

"Don't let this place fool you. There's no money, and the bloody stables don't make a thing. The only thing of any real value for Clive and me was that bloody folio."

"And when did you realise it was in the totem pole?"

Simon looked at Brock in surprise. "You seem to be quite on top of your game, Inspector. Yes, I guessed the bloody thing was in there. It's just the kind of sick joke my father would play. Give the thing to that idiot Ted Daley and then let him use the money to buy the estate out from under us."

"You think he would have bought the estate?" Poole asked.

"Of course he bloody would. The man loves the place for some reason."

"And you don't?"

He looked at Poole, his eyes narrowing. "This place has been like a prison to me."

"So you contacted Matt Pike to try and sell the folio before Ted Daley found it?" Brock asked, trying to steer them back on track.

"I knew Ted wouldn't find it. The only thing that man has between his ears is more of the dung he spreads on the roses. I was more concerned that once it got to the museum, I wouldn't have a chance to do anything. The bloody idiot donated it so quickly I barely had time to get the thing out."

"You did though, didn't you?"

"Not exactly, no." He sighed and leaned back in his chair. "I called Matt up and told him to get over on Thursday afternoon, as it would be the last chance we had to get it out and away. He turned up, and we went down to the barn."

"Where were your house guests?"

"Off on the ride. I'd suggested it so I could head straight back to the barn and hand over the folio to Pike before they got back."

"What went wrong?" Brock asked.

Simon shook his head. "I don't know. Pike arrived, we opened the panel, and the folio was there. Matt said that we'd need something to pick it up with and something to put it in. He said it was so old it was likely to crumble if we just carried it. I went back up to the house to grab some tissues and a big plastic bag to put it in."

"And then?"

"By the time I got back, Pike was gone."

"Gone? You mean he was dead when you returned?"

"No, I mean he was gone. I thought he'd bloody scarpered with my inheritance."

Poole frowned and turned to Brock, whose brow was also knotted.

"And there was no sign of the folio?"

"Well, of course, there wasn't, he'd bloody taken it!"

"And was the panel still open on the totem pole?"

"No, it was back in place."

"And you didn't open it again?"

"Of course not, he was hardly going to have put the bloody folio back in there, was he? Anyway, I had to get back up to the house for when the others got back."

"So how do you explain how Matt Pike ended up dead and stuffed inside the totem pole?"

Simon Pentonville stared back at Brock. "I can't explain it, but it had nothing to do with me. I met with the others back at the house."

"And how was your brother involved in all this?"

Simon leaned back on the desk, his eyes down. "He wasn't. He'd gone to London. I don't know how he ended up on the estate the way he did."

"You realise how this looks, don't you?" Brock said after a few moments of silence. "You tried to sell off something that didn't belong to you and the man you were selling it through was killed. Then your brother, who may well have fought you for that inheritance, was killed."

"I know exactly how it looks, that's why I kept my mouth shut," Simon said, sounding desperate. "But I swear I had nothing to do with either of the murders. Nothing."

"Who else knew about the folio?"

"Everyone's heard of it around here, but it was a legend, not something real."

"Did you know that Lucy Flowers has been selling off some of the items in the barn?"

Brock delivered this information without warning, and the shock on Simon's face was plain to see.

"That little...! So she killed Pike? She's got the folio?"

"Funnily enough, they're not admitting to anything."

"It has to have been them. I want you to search their houses. One of them must have the thing."

"Maybe, maybe not. Right now we don't have anything concrete tying them to the murders. Let's not forget, Mr Pentonville, you were the only one who was in contact with Matt Pike, you invited him here."

"But I didn't kill him!" Simon shouted, his right fist hitting the desktop hard.

Poole felt his phone buzz in his pocket and pulled it out to see Sheila's name. He got up and moved into the hallway. As he did so, someone vanished back into the dining room on the opposite side, but he didn't see who.

"Sheila? What's up?"

"We've matched the blood on the crowbar from the museum with both victims. It looks like Matt Pike and Clive Pentonville were both killed with the same weapon."

"Sorry," Poole said, his head spinning. "You're saying that the crowbar has Clive Pentonville's blood on it as well?"

"Yes. Why? Is that significant?"

"Just a bloody bit! Thanks, Sheila." He shoved the phone back in his pocket and leaned back through the door of the study.

"Sir?"

Brock caught his expression and made his way out into the hallway.

"What is it?"

"Sheila's matched the blood on the crowbar to Matt Pike."

Brock took a deep breath. "We need to talk to Frazer again."

"Hold on though, she's also matched blood on it with Clive Pentonville."

"What?!" Brock grunted in surprise.

"This must mean that even if Matt Pike was killed at the museum, Clive Pentonville wasn't," Poole said. "The killer's hardly going to kill him there and bring the body all the way back here."

"Whereas Matt Pike could well have been killed here along with him, just like we first thought," Brock added.

"But why would someone kill them both there and then take the crowbar to the museum?"

"To throw us off the bloody scent, Poole," the inspector growled. "And it worked. Think about it, that break-in was conveniently the night the pole arrived at the museum."

Poole frowned. "So the only reason to break into the museum was to make us think that the murder of Matt Pike had happened there?"

"And then that little plan went wrong when Frazer lied about them getting into the actual museum."

The door to the study opened, and Simon Pentonville emerged, glowering at them.

"Am I supposed to wait here all day?"

"We'll get back to you," Brock said before turning and walking out through the main door.

Poole followed him, catching up as the inspector moved quickly across the gravel drive with his long stride.

"So, we don't think Simon Pentonville was involved now?"

"I'm not saying that," Brock said, "I just need to think,

and that posh idiot whining wasn't going to help."

"So, we think the killer guessed that the body would be discovered in the museum. And broke into the place to make us think that it had happened there, only that plan went wrong when Frazer lied about the fact they'd actually got in?"

"That and the fact they brought something with them when they broke in," Brock said as he turned off the driveway and around the side of the house.

Poole stopped as something clicked in his brain. "You mean they took the crowbar and left it there so that the murder weapon would be discovered in the museum with the body?"

"And we'd suspect someone there."

The anger in Brock's voice left Poole in no doubt that he was thinking of Laura, and how whoever had committed these murders had put her directly in the firing line.

They had walked down the long, grassy slope and were now approaching the stables.

"Wait a minute, what about the crowbar we found here by the barn?" Poole asked, remembering how Brock had been curious about where they had found the crowbar.

"I bloody knew that was odd. No one leaves a crowbar out lying on the grass when the barn where it's supposed to be stored is only a few feet away."

"But where did that crowbar come from?"

Brock stopped and turned to him.

"Go on."

"Well if the killer used the crowbar from the barn to kill both Clive Pentonville and Matt Pike, then where did this one come from? Didn't Lucy Flowers and Ted Daley say there was only one on the grounds?"

"Bloody hell. Yes, they did."

"And if the one in the museum is the murder weapon and

was taken from here, where's the one in the museum?" Poole continued.

Brock stared at him.

"They bloody swapped it! The killer took the murder weapon to leave it in the museum. When they got there, they must have seen the other one and couldn't believe their luck!"

Poole grinned; this was progress.

"Good work, Poole." Brock slapped him on the shoulder and almost drove him into the ground. "So now all we have to do is—" The inspector paused and looked at the ground. "Why didn't they put the crowbar back?"

"Sir?" Poole said, not following.

"When the killer got the crowbar from the museum and came back here, they must have been doing it so that the one here wouldn't be missed, and they were coming back here of course."

"Coming back here?"

"Oh, come on Poole, whoever killed these two men must have been on the estate. We're either looking at one of the people staying at the house or Lucy Flowers."

"Not Frazer?"

"He's hardly going to try and set himself up, is he? Anyway, my point is, if they were bringing the crowbar back to swap them, why didn't they leave it in the barn?"

"So we can rule out Simon Pentonville and Lucy Flowers. They both had keys." Poole had trailed off as he had spoken and he stared into the distance now, his mouth open.

"What is it?" Brock asked.

"What was it you said just now? That Frazer wouldn't exactly set himself up?"

"Yes, why?"

Poole's eyes focused as he turned to the inspector. "I think I know who the murderer is."

CHAPTER THIRTY-FOUR

Poole jogged across to where the stable girl he had spoken to previously was standing. She was brushing the mane of a large chestnut horse that was silently munching on hay in a high basket.

"Excuse me," Poole said as he approached.

"Oh! Hello again. Do you need me to come down to the station and make a statement?!" she said excitedly, flashing the braces which covered her teeth. "I know you don't ride in a normal police car because you're detectives, but does yours have a siren? Can we put it on?"

All this had been delivered so quickly that Poole hadn't had a chance to interrupt her, so when there was this slight pause, he seized it.

"Can you tell me if one of the horses here is injured?"

"Injured? Well, Sky down there's had a dodgy leg, yeah."

"Damn it!" Poole said, wheeling away from her.

"What is it, Poole?"

"Oh, it doesn't matter, I'm wrong."

"Even wrong ideas can help sometimes," Brock answered. "Come on, what is it?"

"Well, you said that Frazer wouldn't set himself up, and I suddenly thought about what had set us on his trail in the first place. It was Helen Blaxon's description of someone who looked like him on the grounds of the manor."

"Right." Brock nodded.

"Now he says he was never here, so just suppose we trust him on that? Then that means Helen lied, and if she lied about that it would only be to implicate Frazer."

"Which means she could have been the one to try and frame him with the crowbar as well," Brock continued.

"And could have been our murderer: that is, until I checked her story," Poole said miserably, jerking his thumb behind him where the stable girl was still listening intently.

"You were checking whether her horse really was injured on Thursday or whether she just rode straight back and could have committed the murder while the others were on their ride?"

Poole nodded and kicked a small stone across the stables.

"Did you say Thursday?" the girl said from behind them.

"Yes?" Poole said, turning back to her. "Why?"

"Sky's had that bad leg at least a couple of weeks, she didn't hurt it on Thursday."

The two men turned as one and marched off towards the Manor House.

"Did I help?" the girl shouted after them, but neither turned around.

CHAPTER THIRTY-FIVE

J ust minutes later, they headed through the still open door of Otworth Manor and moved towards the sound of voices coming from the dining room.

"Where is Helen Blaxon?" Brock said as soon as he had entered the room and had seen that only Simon Pentonville, Jonathan Finley and Ellie Kendall were present.

"We were just asking the same thing," Ellie laughed. "No one's seen her for a couple of hours."

Brock turned his head to one side and muttered, "Call for backup, Poole."

Poole nodded and stepped a foot back into the hallway to make the call.

"What do you want with Helen?" Jonathan said, standing up from the table and staring at the inspector.

"On the afternoon that you all took a ride, Helen Blaxon said her horse had injured itself, is that correct?"

"Yes, why?"

"Because none of the horses in the stable have been injured recently, Mr Finley."

"What the bloody hell's that got to do with anything? It was probably just a light sprain and the blasted animal walked it off!"

"Or Helen Blaxon lied."

"Why on earth would she lie about a thing like that?!" Ellie chuckled. "All seems a bit silly to me."

"Bloody ridiculous," Jonathan Finley said angrily.

"If she had lied about the horse being injured," Brock continued as Poole returned to the room, "then she could well have been at the barn when Matt Pike was killed."

"Why on earth would she kill this Pike person?!" Ellie brayed.

"Possibly because he had an incredibly valuable artefact with him."

"Oh, bloody hell," Simon said quietly. He slumped down in his seat and stared blankly ahead.

"What is it, Simon?" Finley asked, looking between his friend and the police. "What are they talking about?"

"Oh!" Ellie squealed suddenly. "You're talking about this Shakespeare book, aren't you?! Is it really real?!"

"Yes, Miss Gould," Brock answered steadily, holding her eye. "I believe it is."

"And you think Helen's scarpered with it! How exciting!"

"Shut up, Ellie!" Simon shouted at her before getting up and moving to where the inspector was standing. "Do you think Helen killed my brother?" He spoke through gritted teeth with barely controlled anger.

"We can find out if we can speak to her. Did she leave in her car?"

"No," Simon said, his eyes widening. "No, I checked, and it was still here. That means it's either still on the estate or she's trying to leave on foot." He turned and ran into the corridor, and the other four bundled after him.

"We've already looked through the house," Simon said as they caught up with him on the steps of the house. "She must be out there somewhere."

"Oh, come on Simon, this is ridiculous!" Jonathan said. "Helen wouldn't have had anything to do with all this!"

"Finley," Simon said. "You're a good bloke, but you're a bloody idiot."

"Hey!" Jonathan said, pulling Simon's shoulder back so the two men were face to face. Their angry faces were just inches from each other.

Brock and Poole ignored them, their eyes scanning the grounds of the estate which spread out before them. Sirens sounded in the distance, gaining in volume.

"We have people on the way," Poole said, "we'll find her. I think it's best you all go inside and wait in the dining room."

"You're going to search the place?" Ellie asked.

"Of course they are," Simon Pentonville said. "And keep us cooped up in the house like useless animals while they do it." He turned away from Finley and looked out across the estate, breaking the tension between the two men.

"Oh, come on, let's go and have a drink," Ellie said. The other two grunted but followed her back into the house.

Poole looked at his watch. "It's only bloody ten thirty."

"Don't knock having a drink before midday, Poole," Brock grumbled as he watched two police cars turned into the long drive. "I'd bloody murder for one right now. Let's make sure they're all behaving, shall we?"

They headed back into the house and found Simon and Jonathan sitting sullenly, both sipping at large measures of whiskey.

"Where's Ellie?" Brock asked.

"Gone to get a lime for the drinks," Simon answered.

"When you find that little bitch Helen, I want my inheritance back."

"And your brother's killer brought to justice, of course?" Brock said, an eyebrow rising.

"Well, yes," Simon said, taking another gulp of whiskey.

The sirens were louder now, and Brock nodded to the door. "You'd best go and get everyone up to speed."

"Yes, sir," Poole said, and headed back outside.

The two squad cars were just pulling to a halt in front of the steps to the house as he came through the door. He saw Sanita flash a quick smile at him through the window of the first car before she stepped out, with Davies climbing from the other side.

"We've got something in the case?" she said as she jogged up the steps.

"We think so," Poole answered. "Helen Blaxon, one of the guests here. She lied about her whereabouts at the time of the murders and now we can't find her. We need to search the whole..." He paused as a movement from the far side of the driveway caught his eye. A woman was running along the edge of the grass and heading towards where the row of 4x4s had been parked for the last few days.

He shouted to the officers of the second car who were only just getting out of their car, as they were closest, and began running down the steps.

The woman looked over her shoulder, and her blonde hair flashed in the sun. Poole realised with a jolt he was watching Ellie Kendall and not Helen Blaxon. She turned away from him and climbed into the end vehicle and fired up the engine. Since he wouldn't catch her on foot, Poole checked his run and darted right towards the second squad car.

To his left, Ellie Kendall darted the vehicle forward onto the grass and then swung hard right, passing around the other cars and bouncing onto the long driveway away from the house.

Poole shoved an officer out of the way and headed for the driver's door, but was cut off by Sanita who dived in ahead of him. Without breaking stride, he ran around the front and climbed in the passenger seat.

"Sorry, sir," Sanita said as she started the engine and skidded the car backwards in reverse. "But I'm a trained pursuit driver."

"Fine with me, just bloody catch her!" Poole said, his hand reaching up and grabbing the handle above the door.

"So, this is Helen Blaxon?" Sanita said once they were on the drive and heading after the 4x4 in the distance. "Where did she come from?"

"No, it's Ellie Kendall. She was in the house a minute ago."

"Why is she running?" Sanita asked as she reached top gear and floored the accelerator.

"No idea, but I think we'd better find out," Poole shouted above the scream of the engine as Sanita barrelled it down the narrow driveway.

They were gaining on Ellie, but she had had a head start and was closing in on the gate that led out of the estate.

Poole pulled his phone from his pocket and saw four missed calls from Brock. He called him back.

"Poole, what the bloody hell is going on?" Brock shouted as soon as he had put the phone to his ear.

"Ellie Kendall's doing a runner."

"I gathered that much from the uniform whose car you stole. I'm in a car behind."

Poole frowned. Brock had never driven as far as he knew, but he had never found out why. He grinned as a sudden realisation came to him. "Bloody hell, is Davies driving?"

"Yes," came Brock's rather strained voice. "So make sure you catch this bloody woman soon or there may well be another death. I've left uniform to call for more backup and secure the house, but something tells me that Helen Blaxon isn't going to turn up anymore."

"You think Ellie Kendall's done something to her?"

"You don't run for nothing. I think she knew we were about to search the place, and so decided to get out before we found whatever it is she doesn't want us to find."

"She's gone left," Sanita said, swerving the car slightly to avoid a pothole as they approached the gate.

"She's gone left, sir," Poole repeated into the phone.

"OK," Brock said. "I'm going to hold on tight and hope that Davies manages to go through the gate and not drive us into the estate wall."

The line went dead as Sanita slowed the car as they passed through the gate and turned left.

"Is Davies any good at driving?"

"He's actually better than you'd think," Sanita answered.

This was a relief to Poole, who had never seen Davies stand up for more than five minutes without knocking something over. He turned around to see Brock's car fly out of the gate behind them before turning back to the 4x4 that was ahead of them along a narrow road running alongside the wall of the estate.

"What's the plan here?" Poole asked.

"Not a clue," Sanita answered. "The roads around here are pretty narrow so I doubt I'll be able to get in front of her even if I do catch her."

Laburnum trees line the road, their yellow flowers

shining in the sunlight as the two cars raced along the empty road through the shadows of the leaves which danced around them.

"Can we get someone to cut her off?"

"I doubt it, there's a maze of little roads around here. As soon as we tried to direct someone in front of her she could take one turn and end up miles away."

Poole stared at the back of the car in front that they were now only a short distance from. "I guess she'll run out of petrol, eventually?"

Sanita laughed, and Poole felt a strange tingle of happiness. Despite the breakneck speed and clear danger of the situation, he was somehow enjoying the fact he was experiencing it with Sanita.

"She's slowing down," Sanita said, her foot moving to the brake. "She's giving up."

Poole unclipped his seat belt, ready to jump from the car when the 4x4 in front lurched suddenly to the right and entered a field.

"Oh bloody hell," Sanita muttered before swerving the police car in after it.

Their wheels bounced through the large rivets left by farm vehicles and Poole's head hit the roof.

"She thinks she can outrun us going cross-country," Sanita shouted as she wrestled with the wheel.

"I think she's probably right," Poole answered as he tried to shield his head with his right arm while holding on to the handle with his left.

"No chance."

Poole looked at her and noticed she was grinning, with a look on her face he hadn't seen before. Like a fox who had just seen a rabbit. He smiled too.

The field in front of them had a sharp slope to their right, leading down to a small stream. On the other side of the stream was another field that rose upwards. Poole saw a gate on the other side and a car pass it.

When he looked back to Ellie, he saw what she was doing. There was a gentle slope ahead of them which turned right towards the stream at the end.

"There's a road on the hill up on the other side of the stream. She might be heading for that."

"Damn it, she is," Sanita answered. "She's banking on us not being able to make it across the stream."

Poole saw her turn her head and look to her right.

"No!" he said suddenly, realising what she was about to do.

"We're going to have to cut her off, it's the only way!"

"Oh, bloody hell!" Poole braced his feet against the back of the footwell as Sanita swung the car to the right and plunged them down the steep slope.

The car bounced downwards at a violent speed. Poole clamped his mouth shut so he didn't scream in front of Sanita, who was still wearing the maniacal look of someone who was thoroughly enjoying herself.

The car slid right and then left as Sanita fought to keep control. Poole looked out of his window and saw Ellie Kendall's 4x4 reach the bottom of the gentle slope and turn right, heading towards the small stream. He realised she would beat them across before they reached the bottom.

"We're going to have to go faster!" he shouted above the sound of the long grass scraping the bottom of the car. Quickly wondering why on earth he would say such a thing, even if it were true.

The car lurched forward as Sanita gave up trying to control the car and instead hit the accelerator. The car took off as it hit a small bump which lifted it upwards before crashing back down again. Poole closed his eyes as they bounced from one divot to another, becoming airborne in between for seconds at a time.

"Here we go!" Sanita shouted.

Poole opened his eyes to see the 4x4 flash past before a piercing crunch of metal sounded and their car swung violently from the impact into its rear.

They skidded to a halt facing back up the hill. To their left, they watched as the 4x4 finished its own spin by hitting a large boulder which was embedded into the bank of the stream. The vehicle lifted and slowly toppled sideways into the water.

"Are you OK?" Poole said as he unclipped his seat belt.

"Fine," Sanita answered, following suit.

They climbed out and ran across to the 4x4 as the second squad car pulled up behind theirs and Brock and Davies stepped out.

Poole looked through the windscreen of the 4x4 and saw Ellie Kendall lying on the driver's door, the water slowly filling around her. He climbed up the underside of the car using the wheel arches as foot and hand holds, opened the passenger door and climbed down alongside her. He felt her pulse and, satisfied she was still alive, lifted her head gently out of the rising water before turning back to the windscreen in front of him.

Brock, Sanita and Davies all stood there watching him.

"Stand back!" he shouted, and they all moved back a few feet. He wedged his back against the metal frame of the cab and kicked out at the glass in front of him. It took five hard kicks before the glass pushed out into the stream and the others rushed in to help him remove Ellie from where she lay. Davies and Sanita carried her out and laid her on the bank.

Poole had half stepped out of the vehicle when he heard

a scuffling noise behind him. He turned back into the vehicle and leaned over to the back seats and looked down at the small form of Helen Blaxon. Her hands tied, her mouth gagged, and a small trail of blood running down her forehead from a deep wound.

CHAPTER THIRTY-SIX

"No! I won't allow it!" Jonathan Finley bellowed, his face contorted with rage.

He had stepped towards Brock, chest out and breathing hard with anger as they faced each other in the hospital corridor. Constable Davies hovered to one side of them, unsure whether he should be restraining the man or not, Poole to the other.

"She's been in an accident! You can't just come in here and start questioning her!"

"I'm afraid we can, Mr Finley," Brock said. He was standing in front of Finley, unmoved by his aggression, by the cool, grey eyes staring back at him. "The doctor's given us the all-clear to talk to her, and Miss Blaxon is a suspect in a murder inquiry."

"A suspect?! What are you talking about? It's bloody Ellie you need to lock up; she's the one who almost killed Helen!"

"Ellie Kendall is in custody and we'll deal with her in good time, but before that, we need to speak to Miss Blaxon."

Finley turned away and roared as he threw a coffee cup into the bin and stormed off down the hospital corridor.

"Keep an eye on him, Davies, and whatever you do, don't let him come in this room."

"Yes, sir," Davies answered, looking mightily relieved that the possibility of him being called into action against Jonathan Finley seemed to have passed.

Brock and Poole stepped into the private room where Helen Blaxon was sitting on a bed, her eyes wide with fear.

"Well this is a right mess you've gotten into, isn't it, Miss Blaxon?" Brock said. "First, you start off by lying to us during a murder inquiry, next thing you know you're tied up in the back of a car rolling into a stream. Not your week, is it?"

She swallowed, but said nothing, her eyes wide and rimmed with tears. A large dressing was taped to one side of her head, a dark-red stain already seeping through the white padding.

"You need to tell us what happened," Brock said softly. "Otherwise we won't be able to help you in how this is all going to progress."

Helen Blaxon nodded and wiped her eyes. "I'll tell you everything."

CHAPTER THIRTY-SEVEN

"You might as well tell us everything, Ellie," Brock said. "We know most of it now, anyway."

Ellie looked at him with the same smirk she had had every time they had seen her. This time, though, Poole saw something different in it. Previously he had seen it as nothing more than a quirk of a slightly simple woman. Now he saw something more sinister there. Something more malevolent.

They were in an interrogation room at Bexford Police, and the silence hung heavy in the air. The only noise was from the low hum of the yellow fluorescent strip lights above. None of this seemed to worry Ellie though, who was sitting, relaxed, and smiling back at them.

"Helen is fine by the way," Brock continued. "She's got a bump on her head and she's probably going to prison for helping to cover up the murders, but other than that she's fine." He leaned back and placed his hands behind his head, his fingers interlocked.

"She told us how you and she decided to cheat at the

horse ride. That you both doubled back towards the manor house as soon as you'd left the others. But when you got there you saw Simon, didn't you? You wondered what he was doing there and so you both followed him down to the barn. You know? It's funny. Helen's story about her horse being injured had sounded plausible; we didn't even think to question it until it was almost too late. We were forgetting that you'd given us an excuse as well. It didn't occur to us because you were clever enough to make your lie occur before the horse ride. What was it again? That you'd forgotten something back at the house? That's when you said you'd seen Clive Pentonville, implicating him. That was nonsense though, wasn't it? In fact, you've been giving us so many misleading threads it's a wonder we ever unravelled the truth."

Ellie looked across at her lawyer, who was sitting making notes, and then back to Brock.

"So there you are, near the barn, and you see Simon," he continued. "Helen and you were congratulating yourselves for being oh-so-funny by cheating at the race, but then you saw him. I'm sure at first you thought he'd had the same idea as you, eh? That he just wanted to cheat at the race? But then you realised something else was going on. He was meeting someone. Matt Pike, to be precise. You both decided to sneak into the barn, hide and listen.

"And that's where you saw your opportunity, isn't it? You heard them talk about the Shakespeare folio and you saw your chance to solve your financial problems in one go. I bet you couldn't believe it when they opened the pole, and the thing was actually in there, let alone when Matt Pike sent Simon off to the house to get something to store it in. You must have thought all your Christmases had come at once."

He leaned back and took a deep breath. "Now, this is

where it gets a little bit tricky. You see, Helen says that you went mad at that point, ran forward and hit Pike over the head with the nearest thing you could find: a crowbar."

Again, Poole tried hard to not let his face betray any emotion. Just an hour before he had been sitting with Brock as Helen Blaxon had told them a different story. That Matt Pike had been about to steal the folio, sending Simon up to the house to get him out of the way. The inspector was testing her, hoping to make her confess by protesting the inaccuracies.

She said nothing.

"See, I think it might have been different," Brock continued. "I think Pike might have been about to steal the thing and you realised if you let him take it off the estate, then you would never get your hands on it. So you hit him." Brock leaned forward again and looked into her blue eyes. "I wonder? Did you mean to hit him that hard?" He held her unblinking gaze for a moment before leaning back again. "Either way, you and Helen realised he was dead almost immediately. Helen panicked, or so she says." He shrugged. "She told us she was crying, shouting, freaking out, told us you were cool as a cucumber. You told her to go up to the house, fake the horse injury and keep Simon up there a bit longer." Brock waited for a beat, again hoping to get a rise from Ellie, but she remained silent, leaning back and folding her arms.

"That was when you decided to tuck away the folio, just in case, eh? And now we come to the part of the story where you met Clive Pentonville and where we get a bit hypothetical. I think you decided to stuff the body in the totem pole, seal it up again and then keep Helen quiet, probably by killing her, so that you could sell the folio and keep the profits. Is that when Clive stumbled across you? Just as you were disposing of Matt Pike? What I don't understand is how you managed to deal with Clive and finish the clean-up of Matt Pike at the same time?"

"Do you know, Inspector? I think you're really quite clever. You've made all these clever guesses about what happened and now you're trying to make me think that Helen told you all of that."

"What makes you think she didn't?" Brock asked.

"Because I know Helen. She's a frightened little thing with no backbone."

"Unlike you, you mean?"

She looked at Brock and smiled. "Yes, Inspector, unlike me. If you want to get on in life you must grasp opportunities, that's all I did."

Ellie's lawyer put her hand on her arm to stop her speaking and she gave a small laugh.

"Don't you think it's funny, Inspector? All these years I've wanted my father to notice me, to give me just a little part of what I am entitled to? He gave me nothing," she said, suddenly angry. "Now this happens and a fancy lawyer turns up." She turned to the woman next to her. "How much exactly are you bleeding my father dry per hour? I hope it's an absolute fortune!" Ellie gave the familiar braying laugh before turning back to Brock.

"And do you know why he's suddenly loosening the purse strings? It's for the same reason that he hasn't turned up here in my hour of need: Because he's ashamed of me. He wants this awful little mess to go away, to brush it under the carpet." She smiled, her eyes burning brightly. "Well, I'm not going to give him the satisfaction. I'll tell you exactly what happened, Inspector."

"Miss Kendall, I really must advise that you don't say another word," the lawyer said sternly, her brow knotted in concern.

"Oh, I don't think you can get me to do anything. Nobody controls me. Inspector, you were right that Clive turned up just as I was getting that horrible greasy man from London into the totem pole. It was a funny thing to do, I see that now, but it seemed to make so much sense at the time. I knew the pole had been checked and nothing found in it, Simon had told me, so I knew no one would open it again for a good while. When this horrible man told Simon to go and get some bag or other I knew what he was up to straight away, maybe he was a little like me? Takes one to know one and all that!" She laughed again before continuing.

"When I realised he was going to run away with the bloody thing, I knew I had to stop him. I'd found the crowbar leaning against the shelves where Helen and I were hiding, I picked it up, ran out and hit him with it. It was strange," she said, her head tilted to one side, frowning. "There wasn't as much blood as I thought. Anyway," she said, shaking her head slightly. "I told Helen to get off up to the house and stall Simon while I sorted it all out. She's such a timid little thing, it was quite easy to have her thinking the whole thing was her fault! Then I shoved him in quickly and put the panel back on. The thing was so tight I had to bash it back in with the crowbar, but I managed it. It was then I turned round to see Clive standing, watching me. I think he was in shock as he hadn't said anything, just standing there with his mouth open!"

"And so you turned the crowbar on him, too?"

"Oh no, not just like that. The totem pole was full. Where would have I put him?! I knew I had to deal with him as well though, but how to get him away? I knew Simon would be back at any minute." She grinned at them. "Can you work it out, Inspector? It was awfully clever of me, really."

Brock exhaled slowly and leaned forward. "The body was found a good quarter of a mile away. It seems unlikely you dragged him there without anyone seeing."

"Dragged him?! Oh, Inspector, you are funny!" Ellie roared with laughter again.

Poole felt an unpleasant, sick feeling in the pit of his stomach watching her. She was strangely detached from the situation in which she found herself, and even from what she had done.

"Clive went to the copse of his own accord," Ellie said smugly.

"How did you make him go there?" Poole asked.

"I told him his brother had killed that horrible man." She shrugged. "I said that Simon had killed him and I'd sent him up to the house to clean up and then dig a grave to put the body in. I told him that we would buy the pole from the museum before it ever left the estate and then bury the crowbar with the body and nobody would ever know the difference."

"And he believed you?" Brock asked.

"Do you know? I don't think he did. But then I played my trump card!" She laughed, eyes shining.

"Which was?"

"I showed him the Shakespeare folio, obviously. His eyes almost burst out of his head! Once he'd seen that, and I told him that this man had tried to steal it from Simon, he bought it all. I told him Simon was going to bury the man in the copse and that we should go and help him. No one was going to find the body in the meantime. He agreed, and we walked over there. Easy as anything, apart from him making a bloody phone call, that was a sticky moment!"

"He called Byron Lanister to try and buy the pole?"

"Yes, I didn't think he'd go and do it right there and then. Everyone thought he had gone off to London, so I was just going to pretend I'd never seen him."

"And why hadn't he gone to London?"

"Do you know? I never found out. But I suspect he came back because he'd suddenly had the same thought as Simon had. That the Shakespeare folio was real and was hidden in the totem pole. He always was a little slower on the uptake than Simon. He didn't even twig something was wrong when I took my horse across to the woods with me—I think he was still in a daze."

"And what happened when you got to the woods?" Brock asked.

"I really insist that you don't say another word!" Ellie's lawyer said loudly.

Ellie turned to her slowly, rising in her seat, her head rising on her long neck. "I have already told you, you don't tell me what to do. Nobody does." A chill ran around the room. Ellie's words had been quiet, forceful, and full of malice.

She turned back to the inspector, the vague grin returning. "I hit him over the head, Inspector; surely you must know that from having seen the body? I'm afraid there was a lot more blood this time, I must have hit him differently." She shrugged. "Anyway, I covered him up and made it back to the house on horseback at the same time as Jonathan. He thought I'd just finished the race, of course. Helen was there and said her horse had been hurt, Simon arrived a few minutes later from the stables looking bloody annoyed!" She laughed again. "I'd loved to have seen his face when he got there and that awful Matt Pike had vanished along with his folio."

"What about Simon? I thought you cared for him?" Poole said in disbelief.

"Cared for him?! Oh, isn't he sweet, Inspector?!" She laughed. "You must love having this big puppy dog following you around. No dear," she said in a patronising voice directed at Poole. "Simon was a bloody idiot who I thought was going to inherit a big pile of cash. I wanted in. I was hanging around to see how much it would all work out to, but it was obvious it wasn't going to be much. So, like I said, I took my chance."

"And at what point did you decide to frame Frazer Mullins?" Brock said.

"Do you know, I thought that might have been the cleverest part of all, though I have to say it was pure luck that put me onto it," she answered. "I realised I wouldn't be able to get the body out of the pole and away without others noticing, and then it occurred to me that the best thing would be if I just left him there. There was a small chance that it would be discovered on the way, but I was fairly sure it would make it to the museum in one piece and no one would have any idea he was in there. Then it was just a matter of leaving you a little extra proof, so I slipped something in Simon's drink the night before to make sure he slept well and nipped off to the museum. I grabbed the crowbar from the copse and took it with me. Once I got there, I had just planned to throw the thing into a bin nearby or something, but then I noticed the alley that ran down the back of the building and thought I could do even better. I could make it look like there was a break-in of some kind and then if the body was ever discovered, they'd link it to that. It was all very easy. I smashed the camera with a stone that had fallen from the wall and kicked the doors in. I have to admit I had expected some kind of alarm, but nothing happened." She shrugged.

"If you wanted it to look like a robbery, why didn't you take anything?" Brock asked.

"Because the place was full of junk, Inspector! I had a look around the storeroom, but it was all just a load of old tat, and the last thing I wanted was to actually have to hide more ill-gotten gains. I had the folio already. In any case, it seemed to me that it would look better as a robbery gone wrong if nothing was taken. Then I had a bit of luck in finding a crowbar that was identical to the one I had with me, so I swapped them there and then and got out of there."

"And you couldn't replace the one from the museum into the barn on the estate because you didn't have the key?"

"No, Simon had locked the bloody thing up so I threw it in the grass. I was slightly surprised when you came to the manor to talk to us the next day. I thought you'd stick on the museum angle. You are a clever thing, aren't you?" she said patronisingly.

"I wonder though, how did you come to the conclusion it was Helen? I mean, I had planned for her to take the fall if it came to it, but you caught me off guard turning up again so suddenly like you did."

Brock said nothing for a moment before moving on.

"Poole realised that there wasn't an injured horse."

She frowned and looked at Poole. "Oh, I see!" she said, suddenly smiling. "You realised she'd lied about the horse being hurt and so her timeline of events couldn't be trusted, nor could her identification of Frazer Mullins, am I right?"

Poole nodded.

"Well I must say, I am impressed. I couldn't believe my luck when it turned out that the man Helen had seen weeks ago on the estate worked at the museum. It was quite a turn-up. Of course, we had to use it to push the blame onto him, so I made Helen tell you she'd seen him on the day of the unpleasantness. Then I'd say I'd seen Clive, and you'd put two and two together."

Unpleasantness. That was the word she had used to describe a double murder. Poole felt a shiver run down his spine.

"It seems you saw through my little charade though and were homed in on poor little Helen. I'd realised that this Fraser idea wasn't going to stick, so I decided to pull my last rabbit out of the hat and make Helen 'disappear,' and hope you took that to mean she was behind it. Then, when I was about to make an excuse to drive into town so that I could get rid of her, you turned up and told me you were going to search the whole place. I decided to just make a run for it."

"You honestly thought you would get away?" Poole said, shaking his head.

"No, Detective, I fully planned on being caught, but only after I had disposed of Helen somewhere. Then I would have told you that I had a moment of madness as I'd realised my friend had committed the murders or something like that. You wouldn't have had anything much pointing to me and I have to say, I am rather a good actress." She cackled again and turned to her stony-faced lawyer, who was furiously scribbling copious notes. "I hope you tell my dear father that if he hadn't sent you to my aid, I probably would have kept up the pretence and got away with it. Now he's going to have to live with the notoriety of having a murderess for a daughter." She threw her head back and laughed loudly as the others in the room stared at her in disgust.

"ARE you sure I can't change your mind, Sam?" Chief Inspector Tannock said from behind his large desk. There was no computer on it, just two neat piles of paper and a small bronze statue of a set of golf clubs. He eyed Brock over steepled hands which rested on the end of his bulbous, red nose.

"I'm sure, sir," Brock replied. "I just don't think it's the right time for me to move up the food chain."

Tannock gave a snort of laughter. "Let's not get ahead of ourselves, eh, Brock? You weren't the only one asked to throw their hat into the ring, you know."

"I know, sir," Brock said with a sigh. "I expect Inspector Sharp will be the favourite, sir?"

"Damn fine chap, Sharp. I play golf with him, you know?"

"Yes, sir," Brock answered wearily.

"Ever thought of taking up golf, Sam?"

"No, sir, rugby was more of my game."

"Damn shame, good for the soul, golf. And the career, if you want me to be honest about it."

He stared at Brock for a moment before sighing and shaking his head.

"Very well, if you're sure I'll put it to the top bods that you'd like to withdraw your name from the running for my job."

"Thank you, sir," Brock said, rising.

"Oh, and Sam?"

"Yes, sir?"

"Sharp told me your young sergeant was being disrespectful to him the other day. Mind you keep an eye on that chap, eh? From a criminal background, you know," he said pointedly, looking over his half-rim glasses.

"Yes, sir," Brock answered, jaw clenched and hands

balled into fists as he turned and threw the door of the office open before marching out.

"How did it go, sir?" Poole asked as Brock opened the door to their small office.

"We're going to the pub," Brock snapped, vanishing back into the hallway.

CHAPTER THIRTY-EIGHT

"Are you not drinking?" Sanita asked, her eyes following the elderflower fizz that had been placed in front of Laura Brock.

"No, I'm driving tonight," she answered, smiling.

Poole watched Sanita nod, but with a hint of suspicion in her eye. The police officer in her clearly rising to the fore.

"Another case closed then, everyone," Brock said, addressing the table in front of him, which consisted of his wife, Sanita, Poole and Davies. "Well done all of you, and Davies?"

"Yes, sir?"

"I am never getting in a car with you behind the wheel again as long as I live."

"Yes, sir," Davies said, looking slightly crestfallen.

"I thought he did well, sir—you got there only a little bit after us," Sanita said, grinning.

"The only person I'd want to get in a car with less than Davies here is you, Sanders," Brock said. "At least Davies here had the sense not to drive straight off the bloody hilltop."

Everyone around the table laughed, including Sanita, before she then defended herself. "I was in pursuit; she might have made it across the river if we hadn't got there when we did."

"You're absolutely right, Sanders." Brock raised a glass to her. "Well done. Though I dare say Poole here will be having flashbacks for a while."

The table erupted in laughter again as the conversation turned to news from the manor since the arrest.

"So what's going to happen to the Shakespeare folio?" Laura asked. "That horrible bloody brother isn't going to get it, is he?"

"Doesn't look like it," Poole said. "Apparently the wording of the will listed that Ted Daley would inherit the totem pole and everything in it. No one picked up on the significance of the wording at the time, but it looks like Mr Daley is going to get the folio."

"And is it all right?" Laura asked, clearly concerned about the loss of this piece of British history.

"Yep," Davies said, beaming. "I pulled it out of the glove box when Sanders hit Miss Kendall's car into the river."

"You mean when my skilful driving caught the killer?" Sanders countered.

"Yeah, that." Davies laughed.

Poole pulled his phone from his pocket and looked at it as the others chatted: there were no messages.

It felt strange to be sitting here at the end of a case without his mother tagging along, as she had done before.

"Why don't you ring her?" Sanita said next to him.

Poole looked up, shoving the phone into his pocket. "Sorry?"

"Your mum, call her."

She looked at Poole's surprised expression and laughed.

"I'm not an idiot, you know. I know something's going on with you, and as your mum isn't here, I guess it's something to do with her?"

Poole nodded. "We've got some history that's come between us."

"Well, sort it out," Sanita said in a matter-of-fact voice. "I like your mum and we only get one go at family, so make it count. Call her and tell her to come to the pub."

Poole took a long drink of his pint of Bexford Gold and sighed.

"Oh, come on, whatever it is, it can't be that bad," Sanita said before punching him on the arm. "Call her!"

"All right, all right!" Poole said, smiling. He got up and walked away from the table slightly, where everyone was now discussing Ted Daley's plans to buy the manor house from Simon Pentonville, using the proceeds of the Shakespeare folio.

As the phone at his ear connected, he heard his mother's answering message click in.

"Hi, it's me, Jenny, or Sat Charan if you are using my spiritual name."

Poole rolled his eyes.

"If you want to leave me a message, you can do it after the beep. May the cosmos be kind to you."

"Hi Mum, it's me. We've finished a case so we're at the Mop & Bucket if you want to come for a drink." He hesitated for a moment but couldn't think of anything to say and so hung up.

He stared at the phone, frowning. Despite her constant fear that the signals from the phone were going to melt her brain, he couldn't remember a time when his mother had had her phone turned off.

He scrolled to his contacts and rang the home phone of Angela Hope.

"Hello?"

"Hi Angela, it's Guy Poole here."

"Oh, Guy! Hello! We were wondering when you would call, I'll go and get Debbie right away!"

"No, no!" Poole shouted. "I'd just like to talk to my mum quickly."

"Your mum? What do you mean?"

"Has she gone out?"

"I'm sorry, Guy, I don't know what you're talking about."

"She said she was coming to stay with you for a few days?" Poole said, a sense of dread rising in his throat.

"Well she was, but then she sent me a message saying she'd changed her mind. Is everything OK, Guy?"

"Oh, yes. I'm sure it's fine. If my mum calls you, can you let her know I need to speak to her? Thanks."

Poole hung up and tried to call his mother again. If she hadn't gone to her friend's, where had she gone? She had only been in the area for a short time and outside of Angela, he didn't know of anyone she was close enough to stay with. Even Ricardo, her yoga instructor (and that's all Poole could bear to think of him as), was on holiday abroad.

"Is everything all right, Poole?" Brock said next to him, making him jolt into the present.

"I'm not sure," Poole answered.

Brock frowned at him. He was holding two empty glasses, heading back to the bar for refills. "Let's get another drink and talk about it," Brock said.

"No," Poole said slowly. "No, I think I need to go home."

"Go home? Why? What's happened? Is it something to do with that bloke that was following you?"

Poole looked up at him and swayed backwards slightly. "Oh, bloody hell."

"What is it?"

"Mum said she was going to stay at her friend's but apparently she cancelled by text."

"Right, so she must be staying with someone else. Have you called her?"

"Yes, no answer. Something doesn't seem right," Poole said. "And someone was following me, what if it's something to do with my dad's past again?"

"Call him," Brock said, turning and putting the glasses on a table next to him.

"And say what? Do you know of anyone who might want to hurt my mother because of you?"

"That would be a start."

Poole sighed and lifted his phone. "I'll try her once more."

He called his mother's number and felt a jolt of relief as it connected.

"It's ringing," he said to Brock who nodded, watching him carefully.

The ringtone clicked off abruptly, causing Poole to pull the phone away from his ear and stare at it.

"What's wrong?" Brock asked.

"It went dead after only a couple of rings, like someone rejected the call."

As he spoke, his phone buzzed in his hand. He looked down to see a message from his mother's phone. He opened it and an ice-cold terror gripped his body.

"I HAVE YOUR MOTHER. ONE
DOWN... TWO TO GO."

MAILING LIST

READ on to see the first chapter of the next in series!

MORE FROM A.G. BARNETT

Brock & Poole Mysteries

An Occupied Grave

A Staged Death

When The Party Died

Murder in a Watched Room

The Mary Blake Mysteries

An Invitation to Murder

A Death at Dinner

Lightning Strikes Twice

MURDER IN A WATCHED ROOM

B rock watched with folded arms as Detective Sergeant
Guy Poole paced up and down in front of him. The
dimly lit street shimmered as the light drizzle slanted across
it, as though someone had smudged the world with oil. He
tore his gaze away and surveyed the surrounding buildings,
looking again for any sign of CCTV cameras, but he knew
there were none.

This side street saw little foot traffic, they had to hope
that some of the other residents in the block of flats had seen
something, but his years of experience told him that people
were strangely deaf, dumb and blind when it came to
witnessing crimes. Assuming there had been anything to see
here. They didn't even know if anything had happened
here yet.

Poole stopped his meandering as movement stirred in the
doorway of the building. Sheila Hopkins appeared in her
familiar white suit and Poole dashed towards her.

"Anything?" he asked desperately as Detective Inspector
Sam Brock came up behind him.

"I'm sorry love; we couldn't find anything out of the ordinary. We've taken a load of prints, but let's not get our hopes up." She shrugged. They all knew that whoever had taken Poole's mother was likely to have worn gloves.

Poole nodded and turned away.

Brock exchanged a look of concern with Sheila, who squeezed his arm before heading away to her van.

Brock watched as his young partner wandered aimlessly along the dark street in front of him. Just hours ago they had been with friends, joking, laughing and enjoying a drink in their favourite pub. Now they were here. Shocked, panicked and desolate.

Poole had received a message from his mother's phone that simply read:

ONE DOWN, TWO TO GO...

They had rushed straight back to his apartment, but she had gone. Her purse and handbag were still there, and there were no signs of a struggle. He had no idea what was going to happen next; no idea when or even if they would see Jenny Poole again. All Brock knew was that he had to be there for Poole.

"Come on," Brock said placing one hand on Poole's shoulder. "Come back to ours tonight, there's nothing else we can do here now."

Poole snapped his head towards him, his face suddenly flashing with anger.

Brock prepared himself for a volley of angry words about how they couldn't just stop and go to bed, that they couldn't leave. Instead, though, the young sergeant's body sagged as his eyes, shining with emotion in the dim streetlight, shone. He nodded and turned towards the car with Brock in tow.

They drove in silence. Brock occasionally glanced at Poole, who was driving on autopilot. His eyes glazed as he stared through the windscreen as the streets of Bexford rolled beneath them.

Poole pulled into Brock and Laura's small driveway in front of their modest suburban house and turned off the engine.

"Are you sure it's ok for me to stay?" Poole said in a hollow voice.

"Don't be daft, of course, it is," Brock grumbled as he heaved his large frame from the car. He leaned back in where Poole was still sitting, rigid. "We're going to find her."

Poole nodded. "I know."

Brock headed down the short path to the front door and was relieved to hear the car door open and close behind him. He opened the front door and waited for Poole to enter before closing the door on the chilled night air.

"Oh, Guy!" Laura said, rushing down the hall to him and embracing him. Sanita was next, appearing from the kitchen with a nervous-looking Davies behind her. She took Poole's hand delicately and led him through to the kitchen as Laura and Davies questioned Brock.

"How is he?" Laura asked in hushed tones as she stepped on tiptoes and kissed her husband on the cheek.

"Quiet," Brock rumbled. "Sheila didn't find anything obvious at the flat, but she's taken some prints."

"Wouldn't whoever did it have worn gloves?" Davies asked.

Brock sighed, "Yes, Davies."

He turned and hung his coat on its hook. If even Davies had thought of wearing gloves, he didn't hold out much hope that the kidnapper hadn't thought of it.

"Are you running the case, Sir?" Davies continued.

"We won't be allowed near it, it's too personal. The force doesn't like people getting involved in investigations that involve their own family and friends. Sharp will be running it with Anderson."

"Bloody hell," Davies said, glancing over his shoulder towards the kitchen. "Does he know that?"

"Yes, he threw the mug of tea we'd made him about forty feet down the street when I told him. That's when he went quiet. Come on, I need a drink."

The three of them headed into the kitchen where Poole and Sanita were sitting, her hands wrapped around his right hand as he stared at the table top.

He looked up at Brock as he entered.

"I'm going to make sure we find her, I don't care if it's official or not," Poole said looking him in the eye.

Brock nodded. "I wouldn't expect anything else, but it has to be off the books. In any case, the most important part of this might well be you and your father. We need to go over everything you know, everything that your mum has done or said recently. Anything could be relevant."

"This isn't about anything that happened recently," Poole said bitterly. "This is about what happened all those years ago. This is payback from the drug gang that my family got in the middle of."

Brock felt the tension in the room go up a notch.

On Poole's fifteenth birthday some members of a drug gang had driven past his house and fired indiscriminately into it from the moving vehicle. Poole had been shot in the leg and one of the two friends who had been sharing his big day with him had died. This terrible incident was the culmination of his parent's actions. His father, Jack Poole, for getting caught up in storing and moving drugs for the gang (whether knowingly or not was still up for debate in Brock's eyes), and his mother, Jenny Poole, for approaching the gang and asking them to leave Jack out of it, only to find she had approached the wrong gang and kicked off a gang war that arrived at their house soon after.

The connection between these past events and tonight was obvious; it had been the first thought of Brock and, no doubt, Poole. He knew though that they couldn't get too focused on this. It was all too easy to create your own narrative and fit facts to it rather than allow the facts to present their own conclusion.

"That seems the most likely explanation, but we have to treat this as any other case. Nothing gets ruled out, nothing gets ignored."

Poole nodded and wiped at his eyes.

"Not tonight, though," Brock said. "The official investigation will be gathering everything they can. They've already spoken to both you and your father, there's no more to be done tonight."

Brock watched as Poole wrestled with this, but after a few moments, he nodded.

When they had spoken to Jack Poole earlier, he had been pale and quiet, a mirror image of his son's worry. He had given his statement to the police, patted his son on the shoulder and vanished off into the night with two heavies next to him, promising to put feelers out across his contacts for any news of who had done this, or why. They hadn't heard anything since.

Although Brock didn't want to focus solely on the incident that had changed his sergeant's life all those years ago, he had to admit that he agreed with Poole about the reasons his mother had been kidnapped. People weren't abducted from those on a modest salary such as Poole's, where any ransom would be paltry. These kinds of kidnappings were usually done for revenge and the message Poole had received, sent from Jenny Poole's own phone, seemed to make it clear that the family were being targeted; Jack, Jenny and Guy Poole.

Brock had a sinking feeling that the chances of ever seeing Jenny Poole alive again were slim, but he was determined that her son wouldn't suffer the same fate.